VAMPIRE
ASCENSION

THE VAMPIRES OF ATHENS, BOOK THREE

Eva Pohler

Eva Pohler Books
20011 Park Ranch
San Antonio, Texas 78259
www.evapohler.com

Publisher's Note: This is a work of fiction. Names, characters, places, and incidents are a product of the author's imagination. Locales and public names are sometimes used for atmospheric purposes. Any resemblance to actual people, living or dead, or to businesses, companies, events, institutions, or locales is completely coincidental.

Book Layout ©2017 BookDesignTemplates.com

Book Cover Design by B Rose Designz

Vampire Ascension/ Eva Pohler. -- 1st ed.
Paperback ISBN: 978-0986221446

We're on our own.

—GERTIE

Contents

For my children.

CHAPTER ONE

Not Again

Mamá gasped. "Gertoula?"

The basement of the Angelis's apartment building became very quiet. The joyful noises from their family reunion, from the realization that Phoebe could speak and that Gertie and Hector were safe, and from the blissful feeling of being in one another's arms again came to a halt the moment Mamá noticed that Gertie had not changed.

Gertie was still grappling with it, too. She was trying to convince herself that she was okay. Being human again wasn't necessary to her happiness. She could deal with it. But when she looked into Mamá's horrified eyes, her knees gave out, and she fell to the floor.

"Gertie!"

When was the last time she had fed?

Both Hector and Jeno rushed to her aid, one on each side of her. They looked down at her, their heads nearly touching as the room spun behind them.

"What's happening to her?" Hector asked Jeno. "Why is she still a vampire?"

Nikita and Klaus knelt on the floor beside Hector.

"Does she need a doctor?" Nikita asked. "Jeno, can't you help her? Hector, use your healing powers. Somebody do something!"

"I'm okay." Gertie squeezed Nikita's hand. "Seriously."

Are you going to tell them or should I? Jeno asked her telepathically.

Neither of us needs to say anything. Gertie saw no reason to alert everyone that Jeno was responsible for her becoming a vampire—that Jeno would be the one who'd have to die if she were to ever be human again. What good would it do to tell people that? There was no way she'd ever even consider taking Jeno's life to save her own.

Jeno arched a brow, but she ignored it and sat up.

Before she could say another word, Mamá knelt beside her, too, and said, "You are a part of this family, Gertoula. I won't have you leave us again. No matter what."

Gertie glanced across the room at Babá, who swallowed hard and nodded. "Mamá is right. We were wrong to make you leave. We were afraid—are still afraid—but we will be brave this time."

Holding back tears, Gertie tried to give Babá a smile, but her mouth made more of a frown. As Nikita hugged her, the hairs on the back of Gertie's neck prickled.

Jeno stood up and said to Hector. "They're coming. We need to be ready to fight."

"I'll call for backup." Hector took out his phone and sent a text. Then he opened one of the closet doors and found a sword and scabbard. His thoughts told Gertie that he had stashed them there for emergencies. "Klaus, take your family upstairs."

"Do you have another one of those swords?" Klaus asked.

"No. Why?"

"I want to fight, too," he said.

"You may have to." Jeno grabbed a crowbar from the floor. "They're here."

Babá gathered Nikita and Phoebe in his arms. "Come, Marta. Hide in here."

Just as he opened one of the basement closet doors, Phoebe screamed.

From the top of the stairs, six vampires flew into the room like a flock of giant birds. Gertie's super-human reflexes kicked into gear as she spun around, fists swinging.

Hector drew his sword and decapitated one of the intruders. Jeno clutched the crowbar and drove it, like a wooden stake, through the heart of another. Gertie had no weapon but herself. And Klaus was even worse off, because he had no weapon *and* no extra-human strength. From the corner of her eye, she saw him being pinned against the wall. Euripides stretched open his mouth, fangs protracted.

"No!" Gertie screamed.

Mamá and Nikita also screamed as Babá charged Euripides—like he was any match against a vampire. Euripides tossed him across the room like a rag doll. Gertie shoved the one fighting her and scrambled to Klaus's aid, but the other vampire grabbed her by the ankles and pulled her away. Hector decapitated the one holding her and set her free just as another leapt onto Hector's back and stabbed his fangs in Hector's neck. Gertie pulled the attacker off Hector and hissed as she fought with him. They threw one another against the wall, the ceiling, the floor.

Then Jeno had her attacker by the throat and pinned against the wall. He drove the bloody crowbar through the vampire's chest before turning to Gertie.

"Klaus!" she cried.

Only two vampires remained: Euripides had completely drained Klaus and was holding him like a lover. The other vampire, a female, crouched before them, guarding her clan leader from Hector and Babá, who charged them repeatedly.

Mamá lunged forward. "Don't you dare take another one of my children!" She stood, trembling, before Euripides and his guard. "Take me instead!"

"Mamá, no!" Nikita cried.

Eyes dark and fierce, Euripides stretched open his mouth, his fangs at the ready, but as he went to bite Mamá, Gertie flew in between the two and took the bite in her arm.

Although Gertie couldn't destroy Euripides, her stunt was enough of a distraction for Jeno to move in past the guard, grab the languid Klaus, and flee the basement. Hector, who'd been infected with the virus, flew up and swung his blade toward the guard, but she ducked and followed Euripides up the basement stairs. They went after Jeno and Klaus, as Jeno knew they would.

Hector and Gertie followed, leaving the rest of the Angelis family behind.

Gertie felt the sting of dawn coming as she and Hector found Jeno in the air above Athens shouting at Euripides.

"I'm on your side, you idiot!" Jeno yelled. "My enemy was my father, not you! I was going to come back, to fight with you. And with Lord Hades!"

And I loved my father, but he was wrong, Jeno's thoughts continued.

Gertie's stomach tied into a knot.

"I will never trust you!" Euripides hollered back. "I'll never believe another word you say."

"You need our help," Jeno shouted. "So few of us remain."

"We plan to remedy that tonight," Euripides said. "Now hand over what's mine."

Gertie sensed he meant Klaus.

"Klaus will never be yours!" Gertie screamed. "Read my mind. Jeno speaks the truth. We always intended to help free the vampires."

"Why should I trust a girl who can't even decide which boy she loves?" Euripides sneered. "You and Jeno are better to me dead than alive! Next time, I will kill you myself!"

Hector, who hovered beside her, turned beet red. "Don't talk to her like that!"

"Dawn's breaking," Euripides said. "So you can have the boy for now. But he's mine, and I will be calling for him!" He pointed to Hector. "And you better watch your back. I'm coming for you next!"

The first rays of the sun broke through and stung. Gertie resisted crying out as Euripides and his guard vanished, and she followed the others back to the Angelis's basement.

It took a moment to recover from the stinging burn of her flesh as she sat on the floor between Hector and Jeno, with Klaus barely conscious beside them.

The dawn almost did me in, Jeno said to her telepathically. *I don't think I have much blood left in my body.*

"Klaus!" Mamá rushed to him.

He was weak but awake. "I'm okay."

Two men and a woman the same age as Mamá and Babá descended the stairs.

One of them men extended his hand toward Hector. "Looks like we're too late."

Hector grabbed the man's hand and climbed to his feet. "They'll come back."

"What do we do about Klaus?" Mamá cried with her arms around her son.

Babá joined her. "Is he dying?"

"I'm okay," Klaus insisted again.

"We can turn him," Jeno suggested.

"No!" Babá cried. "Not again. Not another one of my sons. One suffered too long already."

"I don't want to be a tramp," Klaus growled. "If I'm going to die, just let me die."

"This is different," Hector said.

"You support this?" the demigod who had helped Hector up asked him. "What about the law?"

"You have a lot to learn," Hector said without arrogance.

The man gave Hector a look of disapproval.

Gertie climbed to her feet. "If we kill Euripides, Klaus will be restored."

"And we *will* kill him," Jeno said.

"Promise me!" Mamá cried. "Promise me he won't stay a vampire!"

"He speaks the truth," Phoebe said. "It happened to me. We can save Klaus. You've got to trust them, Mamá. Please, Klaus. Let them turn you."

Klaus stared at Phoebe. After a moment, he nodded wordlessly.

Mamá hugged Klaus again before releasing him as tears streamed down her face.

Babá took her in his arms and said to Jeno, "Do what you have to do to save our son."

CHAPTER TWO

Klaus

The three demigods who'd responded to Hector's text promised to return at dusk and station themselves around the building, even though Gertie could tell they had very mixed feelings about allowing Klaus to be turned into a vampire.

"Let's go upstairs," Mamá said once the other demigods had left. "Where we can think."

"The light hurts them," Phoebe said.

"We can close the blinds," Nikita offered. "Won't that work?"

Jeno nodded. "Go ahead. But hurry. Your brother doesn't have much time."

Nikita rushed up the stairs with Phoebe right behind her.

Hector gathered Klaus in his arms, and once Nikita hollered down that they had closed all the blinds, he led the way upstairs to the Angelis apartment. The window in the stairwell had no covering, so the ascent burned, but once they were in the apartment, Gertie took a deep breath and recovered.

"He needs human blood," Jeno said as Hector laid Klaus down on the couch. "He needs it now."

"He can have mine," Hector said.

Jeno shook his head. "Your blood is tainted with the virus."

"What about mine?" Phoebe offered.

"I can tell by your color that you don't have enough," Jeno said.

"Then mine," Mamá insisted. "Let him drink from me."

"Or me," Babá said. "You don't have to be the one, Marta."

"I have done this before," she said.

Babá's eyes grew wide. "What?"

"She can explain later," Jeno said. "We're running out of time."

Mamá extended her wrist, but Klaus only looked at her blankly.

"I can't," he said.

Gertie grabbed Mamá's arm and bit, taking a small sip for herself before pressing the wrist to Klaus's lips. "Please, Klaus."

Klaus was hesitant at first, but then he drank, and the pallor of his complexion diminished with each swallow.

A knock at the door startled them. Gertie could sense her mother on the other side of the door.

The others exchanged worried glances before Babá asked, "Who is it?"

"Diane," Gertie's mother called out. "Have I come at a bad time?"

"She can't see us like this!" Mamá whispered.

"Gertie is her daughter," Babá argued. "She has the right to know."

"Can you come in another hour?" Mamá asked with a strain in her voice as Klaus continued to drink.

"Of course," Diane said. "But is everything okay? You don't sound like yourself, Marta."

The doorknob turned, which, though imperceptible to human ears, was quite audible to Gertie. She dashed across the room to intervene.

As her mother pushed open the door to peer inside, Gertie crowded the narrow opening, even though the light from the stairwell burned.

"Gertie?" her mother asked. Her eyebrows lifted, disappearing behind her blonde bangs. "Oh, Gertie!"

"Please come back later," Gertie said as tears pricked her eyes. She hadn't expected to be overwhelmed with emotion at the sight of her mother. She told herself that it was the sunlight causing the tears, but she knew the truth. She hated this woman and loved her at the same time.

"I've been so worried," her mother said.

Gertie tried hard to hold her tongue before spitting out, "I doubt that."

"Gertoula!" Mamá called from inside. "Don't speak to your mother that way."

Gertie turned to Mamá. "She's not my mother." Her lips quivered as her throat tightened. She wanted to add, *You are*.

Diane turned even paler as she entered the room and closed the door behind her. When she noticed Klaus wiping the blood from his lips and Marta pressing a towel to her bleeding arm, her eyebrows disappeared behind her bangs again. "What's going on?"

"We were attacked," Hector said. "Turning Klaus was the only way to save him."

"I'm so sorry!" Diane said. "This is all my fault."

Gertie wrinkled her brow and asked, "How is this *your* fault? What have *you* got to do with any of this?"

"Oh," Diane placed her hand over her heart.

Gertie sensed she was having chest pains. "Mom?"

"I have so much to tell you, Gertie. I should have told you a long time ago. I'm so sorry."

"I'm listening," Gertie said. "Spit it out."

Gertie didn't wait for her mother to speak. She invaded her mind, seeking answers. Instead, she found confusion and muddled fragments. Seventeen years ago, a handsome man claiming to be a god, a warning, then a prophecy. Maybe if Gertie could lock eyes with her, she could see the past, like she did that time with Phoebe.

"Not now," Jeno said crossing the room to Gertie's side. "Look. I know you're anxious to understand your past, but we have to get Klaus to safety before nightfall."

"Why is Klaus in danger?" Nikita asked.

Mamá covered her face and slouched back in the sofa near Klaus's feet. "I can't take any more of this."

Gertie sensed that Mamá had been able to read Jeno's mind and had learned that Klaus would be controlled by Euripides.

But why hadn't Vladimir controlled Hector? Gertie blocked her mind as soon as the next thought entered: And why hadn't Jeno controlled *her*?

"You and Hector were less susceptible to the manipulation of your maker because you're demigods," Jeno said, as though he had heard *both* of her thoughts. "Phoebe was controlled by Vladimir, through Damien. That's why we couldn't communicate with her. He'd blocked her mind from us and ours from her. She had no choice but to follow his orders."

Phoebe's face turned red as Babá enfolded her in his arms.

"It's okay." Babá patted her head. "You couldn't help it."

"So why couldn't *you* control Damien?" Hector asked.

The mention of his name again brought more tears to Mamá's eyes. Her face went pale.

"I'm sorry," Hector muttered.

"I think my father brainwashed him," Jeno said. "Damien was too young..."

"Stop," Mamá pleaded. "Don't talk about it. I can't take it."

"I don't understand what's going on," Diane said. "Klaus is in trouble?"

"Yes," Jeno said. "The others will wait to attack again tonight, but Euripides can take control of Klaus's mind at any moment."

"So what do we do?" Babá asked.

"We need to restrain him," Jeno said. "And it would be best if we could take him some place far away from here."

"Come to New York," Diane said. "All of you."

Gertie's jaw dropped.

"We can't afford the flight..." Babá started to say.

"I can," Diane said. "I insist. This is my fault anyway. Give me the chance to help."

Gertie still didn't understand why her mother kept saying everything was her fault. She also did not like the idea of leaving Athens. The thought of the Angelis family seeing the luxury of her home compared to their own made her uncomfortable, too.

"What would Dad say?" she asked.

"He doesn't have to know," Diane replied. "He's in Venice. We found a house there."

Gertie searched Jeno's mind to get a sense for his opinion about his mother's suggestion. He wanted them all to go—without him.

"If you stay, so do I," Gertie said to him. She hadn't meant to say it out loud.

"No," Diane said. "If you want to know anything about your past, you have to come, too, Gertie."

"I'll stay here with Jeno," Hector offered. "Maybe we can convince Euripides…"

"If you two are staying, then…" Gertie began.

"No," Jeno interrupted. "Isn't it your duty to protect the Angelis family?" he said to Hector. "Euripides might get to Klaus even as far as New York. The first thing he'll do is make Klaus turn, or kill, his family. You have to be there to prevent that."

Nikita gasped.

"Jeno, you can't stay," Gertie said. "I won't know how to feed in New York."

As Gertie sensed the reproach among the humans, her face turned red. "I can't help it. I have no choice."

She wanted to scream, but she held back. Too many emotions were already filling the room. Her rage didn't need to be added into the mix. "And Klaus will need it, too. How will I do that, Jeno? How will I feed Klaus?"

"Please, Jeno." Marta crossed the room and took Jeno's hand. "Will you do it for me? I'm so frightened for Klaus. We need your help."

Babá frowned.

"I'll help you get settled," Jeno said. "But then I must return to my city." He turned to Hector. "You heard what Euripides said. He plans to make more vampires."

"We need to warn the other demigods." Hector took out his phone. "I'll hold a meeting, come up with a plan."

"Let them handle that," Jeno said. "You go to New York."

"They don't understand," Hector said. "They don't know what I know about your race."

Jeno read Hector's mind. "They despise us. You're worried they will try to exterminate us."

"Exactly," Hector said.

"How soon can you meet?" Gertie asked.

Hector rubbed his chin. "I bet I can get everyone together within the hour."

"We need to bind Klaus with something strong," Jeno said. "The iron chains from the basement."

Klaus's eyes widened. "You want to put me in that coffin?"

"Thee moy. I can't take this!" Mamá cried.

"It would be best if he traveled to New York in it," Jeno said. "It would be safer for him and for us."

Diane took out her phone. "What time should we fly out?"

"How soon can you be ready?" Jeno asked Marta.

CHAPTER THREE

An Impromptu Council Meeting

While Diane remained on her phone upstairs to make their travel arrangements, everyone else returned to the basement. Hector sent out a request for an emergency meeting, calling all available members of the Athens council of demigods to meet in the basement of the Angelis's apartment building within the hour. Meanwhile, Gertie got Hector to help her and Jeno with Klaus.

Jeno and Hector opened Vladimir's tomb as Klaus climbed inside.

He sat up and asked, "You're absolutely sure this is necessary?"

Jeno nodded. "I'm sorry. Just try to think about something else."

Mamá kissed Klaus's hand. "My heart is breaking over this."

"I'll be all right," Klaus said.

"He's a strong boy." Babá patted Klaus on the head but kept his distance. "A man, I mean. Taller than his Babá."

"Read people's minds," Gertie suggested. "It can be very entertaining, right Hector?"

Hector shrugged. "I did it, but I still don't think it's right."

"It definitely crosses a line," Klaus agreed with Hector as he laid back in the coffin.

"Suit yourself," Gertie said. Klaus was probably the most honest person she knew. Of course, he wouldn't read people's minds.

Phoebe peered over the lip of the tomb. "Do what I did. Pretend you're sleeping on the ferry to Crete on the bottom bunk. Those beds feel like tombs, don't they?"

Klaus smiled. "Good idea, Pheebs. Have I told you how happy I am to hear your voice?"

"I'll be sure to talk to you a lot, then," she said. "With your super-human hearing, you'll be able to hear me wherever I am."

"Awesome," he said. "Then I think this will be bearable."

Nikita leaned over and kissed Klaus on the cheek. "I love you. I know I never say it."

"I'm not dying, Nikita," Klaus said.

"Do you have to be dying for me to say I love you?" she asked.

"I guess not." He smiled. "I love you, too. I love all of you."

Then the expression on Klaus's face changed. His smile became a thin line. His eyes lost their focus.

"Euripides," Jeno warned. "He's taken possession."

Klaus glared at Jeno and then sprang from the tomb, clutching Jeno's neck.

Gertie and Hector flew to Jeno's aid as Nikita screamed and Mamá fainted. Klaus forced Jeno back against the wall, knocking down an old lamp and overturning one of the bookshelves. Jeno fought back and pushed Klaus away from the wall, toward the coffin. Hector and Gertie each grabbed one of Klaus's arms, and together they forced Klaus down into the tomb as Babá closed the lid on his own son. Jeno and Hector held the lid down, against the force of Euripides, as Gertie and Babá padlocked the chains. They had barely secured the tomb when they heard footsteps coming down the stairs. Gertie hid the key in the same drawer it had always been kept.

"What the hell is going on down here?" one of the demigods from earlier asked.

As Hector tried to explain, a dozen more demigods—men, women, and teens—entered the basement for the council meeting.

"He's possessed, Cadmon," Hector went on. "But he'll return to normal, once we kill Euripides."

Klaus pounded on the lid of the tomb.

"So why didn't *Gertie* return to normal?" the woman who'd been there earlier asked.

Gertie read Hector's mind to learn her name was Agatha.

Hector glanced at Jeno. "It's complicated."

"Try me," Agatha insisted.

"It was an accident," Hector said. Then he turned to Mamá, who'd been revived from her fainting spell. "Take Phoebe and Nikita upstairs, will you, please, Kiria Angelis?"

Mamá beckoned to the girls. Nikita gave Gertie a frightened glance before leaving with her mother and sister.

"What do you mean by accident?" Cadmon's face fumed with anger.

"Jeno was trying to save his father," Hector explained.

"In order to instigate the uprising against us," Agatha accused.

Hector quickly added, "Jeno didn't know what his father would do."

"Is that why he killed him?" Cadmon's brows lifted. "To stifle the uprising?"

"Not exactly." Hector began to pace. "You all need to understand something."

"You have the virus inside you now," Agatha said. "I can tell by the subtle red tint in your eyes."

"I was bit during the attack," Hector said. "It will wear off soon."

The tension in the room filled Gertie with anxiety. She could sense the distrust among the demigods. Why had Hector called them *here*? They seemed more of a threat than a help.

Hector lifted an open palm in the air. "I understand your concerns, but please hear me out. I called you here for a reason."

"You've been brainwashed by the tramps." Cadmon pointed a finger at Hector. "Haven't you? You've called this meeting to plead the case of the tramps!"

The demigods turned to one another, muttering their questions and concerns.

"We are people, too!" Gertie insisted as she moved beside Hector. "We can't help what we are. We don't deserve to be punished. Punish the victims? That's what you think is right?"

"It's the least of two evils," Agatha clarified. "We have to protect others from also becoming victims."

"The vampires don't want to create more victims," Jeno finally said. "At least, they didn't until recently."

"What is that supposed to mean?" Cadmon asked. "Is that a threat?"

"Not from me," Jeno said. "From a vampire leader known as Euripides. He intends to make more vampires tonight, and we need your help in protecting this city."

"You plan to fight against your own people?" Agatha asked.

"Only until Euripides is destroyed," Jeno replied. "Then I hope to use reason to appeal to the others for a peaceful resolution."

"What's to prevent the others from another uprising?" one of the other demigods asked. "Even after Euripides is gone, another will take his place."

"If we liberate them," Gertie said, "there would be no need for an uprising."

The demigods muttered among themselves as Cadmon and Agatha exchanged looks of concern.

"You want to liberate the vampires?" Cadmon asked Hector.

"They can't keep living like paupers in caves," Hector said. "They need stability and freedom, and we need a system for delivering blood without sacrificing human lives."

"This is preposterous," Agatha said.

"Perhaps Hector needs some time to heal," one of the other demigods suggested. "Maybe he was a tramp for too long."

Someone laughed.

Hector turned red and clenched his fists.

"Jeno broke the law," another said.

"Twice," someone else added.

Gertie spoke telepathically to Jeno and Hector: *We need to get Jeno out of here.*

I'll distract them, Hector said. *Then you two go and hide.*

But the sun, Jeno said. *I can't take anymore. It will kill me.*

The memory of what had happened to Calandra sent a shiver down Gertie's spine. She clutched the locket Jeno had given her—the one that used to belong to his sister.

"We need to take the tramp into custody," Cadmon insisted. "The law is still the law."

"Wait," Hector said. "We need Jeno to stop the others. Let him prove himself to you. Give him a chance. He can redeem himself by defeating the others."

Cadmon seemed to consider this.

"How can we trust him?" Agatha asked. "I don't even trust *you* anymore, Hector."

"You don't have to decide at this moment," Jeno said. "Until nightfall, we vampires are immobile. Think about what you've heard today. You know where to find me tonight."

And if we betray them by going to New York? Hector asked telepathically.

We have little choice right now, Jeno said. *Listen to their thoughts. They want to destroy me. Some want to destroy Gertie, too. They are vampire haters. I don't think you can change that.*

"We need to defend this city together," Hector said out loud. "So please be ready to fight with us against Euripides and his clan tonight. Meanwhile, go home and get some food and rest."

Cadmon turned to Agatha. "What do you think?"

"Let's take a vote," she suggested. "Who here is willing to wait until dusk to reconvene and make our decision?"

"To fight first," Hector interrupted. "Defend the city, and then decide this vampire's fate."

"Saving this city is more important than punishing one vampire," one of the demigods said.

"How do we know the city is at risk?" Agatha pointed out. "These could be lies for all we know."

"I believe Hector," another demigod, about Gertie's age, said. He had red hair and fierce green eyes.

Gertie read Hector's mind to learn the teen's name was Lajos.

"If we ignore their warning and take the tramp into custody," Cadmon reasoned, "we could lose the city. But if we prepare for battle and there is none, then we can always come back for the tramp."

The demigods eventually agreed to prepare for battle, but Gertie didn't breathe again until every last one of them had left the building.

CHAPTER FOUR

On the Run

Gertie's mom was waiting at the door inside the Angelis apartment building when Gertie returned with the others.

"I booked us first-class tickets direct to New York City," Diane said proudly as soon as they had entered. "We leave at three o'clock."

"First class, Diane?" Mamá asked. "Thee moy."

"We wouldn't know the difference, anyway," Babá said with a laugh. "We've never even been on a plane before, have we, my little chickens?" He tickled each of his daughters at their necks and made them giggle.

Gertie glanced at Jeno. Mamá and Hector would be able to tolerate sunlight by then, but how would she and Jeno manage, especially without feeding? Jeno's body could disintegrate, just like his sister's.

"I'll need to go by coffin," Jeno said. "I hope you can get a refund for my airplane ticket, Mrs. Morgan."

Gertie read her mother's mind. No refund and non-transferable, but Diane didn't mind.

"How will we manage that?" Hector asked. "There's no way you can fit in Da…" He stopped himself from saying *Damien's coffin*, recalling Mamá's reaction to the last time he had said her son's name.

Gertie frowned. "And how are we getting Klaus to the airport?"

"I can arrange for that." Diane took out her phone. "I'm Googling funeral homes. I'll pay them well to bring an extra coffin for Jeno in their hearse and to keep their questions to themselves."

What about me, Jeno? Gertie asked him telepathically. *How will I endure traveling in the sunlight?*

You're welcome to share the coffin with me. I wouldn't mind the company.

Gertie smiled. Her mother noticed and took it as a reaction to her management skills.

"I'll do everything I can to fix this," Diane reassured Gertie.

This time Gertie did smile at her mother, even though this was the first time in Gertie's life that her mother seemed to put forth any effort whatsoever. She wondered what had changed.

"The most difficult challenge we face is getting around the demigods guarding the building," Jeno pointed out.

"What?" Hector asked. "Where?"

"Just across the street," Jeno said.

Babá went to the window and peeked through the blinds. "Oh, I see them."

Gertie reached out and sensed them, too. "Just great. What do we do?"

"I can't think on an empty stomach," Babá said, making his way to the kitchen. "I'll cook everyone a nice breakfast so we can sort this mess out."

Gertie didn't have the heart to tell him that vampires didn't like regular food.

"I'm sleepy, Mamá," Phoebe said.

"Let's pack, and then we can eat and sleep until it's time to go," Mamá replied. "Come on, Nikita. You come pack, too."

As the three left the living area for the bedrooms, Gertie wished she could get her things from Hector's house.

"I'll go," Hector said, reading her thoughts. "Once the virus wears off, I'll run home and get your bag and pack one of my own."

"But what will the demigods think?" Gertie asked.

"I'll tell them I'm moving in here for a while," Hector said.

"And then what will they think when we try to leave?" Jeno asked.

They looked at each other blankly for several minutes.

"Think," Gertie muttered.

"We'll tell them the Angelis family has decided to bury Klaus," Hector said suddenly. "And they are leaving for his funeral."

"They'll believe that?" Jeno asked.

"As much as they hate vampires, yes," Hector said. "I can convince them that this family would rather not see their son changed."

"What about me and Jeno?" Gertie asked.

"You really can't take the sun?" Hector asked her. "Even if you're in a car and a plane?"

Gertie sucked in her lips and shook her head.

"I guess I'll have to distract the demigods as you two hide in the other coffin." Hector's face turned a little red—which probably meant he'd overheard Jeno and Gertie's exchange about sharing the coffin. "I'll tell them you're still in the basement, avoiding the sunshine."

"What about you?" Gertie asked Hector.

"I'll sneak away after I get the rest of you safely out of here."

"And if they follow?" Jeno asked.

Hector shrugged. "I don't know."

"I can always come back for you at night," Jeno said. "If you don't make it in time for the flight."

"Sounds good, man."

A few hours later, after some of them had enjoyed Bábá's big breakfast and they had all discussed in more detail the upcoming trip, Diane left for her hotel to pack and Hector felt ready to return to his house for his and Gertie's things.

"Take our car," Mamá insisted.

Bábá took the keys from his pocket and tossed them in Hector's direction. "Be careful, Hector."

"Should I go with him?" Nikita asked.

"That's actually a good idea." Hector turned to Mamá. "I could use another hand, and maybe we'll draw less attention together than I would alone."

"Just two teens running an errand?" Nikita asked.

Hector gave a single nod. "Exactly."

"I don't know," Mamá said. "Is it safe for my Nikita?"

Hector crossed his arms. "The demigods have no reason to be suspicious of her, and the vampires aren't a threat until dusk."

"Go," Babá said to Nikita. "But hurry back."

Gertie's stomach tied in knots as she listened closely to Hector and Nikita make their way to the Angelis car. As was expected, the two demigods stopped and questioned them, and after Hector told his story about temporarily moving in with the family he had sworn to protect, Cadmon said, "As a daughter to Apollo, your mother could never tell a lie. I wonder if that's true of you, too, Hector. You aren't lying to us, are you?"

"Why would I?" Hector said. "I just want to shower and change clothes, man. And Gertie's things are at my house, too. She needs her bag."

They looked at him a moment longer, like sniffing dogs.

"I can't stay in that house," Hector added. "Not with her gone."

They eventually backed off and let him pass. Gertie let out the breath she'd been holding and collapsed beside Jeno on the couch.

This sucks, she said to him, telepathically. *And I'm so hungry.*

Me, too.

Since she could do nothing about her hunger, she sat there, slumped on the couch, obsessively searching Hector and Nikita's minds for any sign of trouble. She sensed Hector thinking more about his mom, about how much he missed her, and about how much he regretted that they didn't spend more time together. Then, much later, after they'd arrived at his house and had begun packing up, she sensed Nikita notice the drawings Hector had done of Gertie, and there was a tinge of jealousy that swept through Nikita's mind.

Jeno noticed Gertie blush. She tried to block him from her mind, but it was too late. He'd already seen her see Nikita looking at the drawings.

Being a vampire can be so complicated, she said to him with a roll of her eyes.

He gave her a smile and kissed her cheek. *It's so much better with friends.*

An hour later, Hector and Nikita returned. They both ran up the stairs, saying the hearse had arrived. Nikita's face was full of fear.

"What about my mom?" Gertie asked.

"She's waiting downstairs with a cab," Hector explained. "She's talking to the hearse driver, too. Paying him extra, I think."

Gertie reached out and sensed her mother.

"Where's my bag?" she asked Hector.

"I loaded it into your mother's cab, along with mine. I told the demigods on guard that your mother was flying home right after the funeral. They assumed the bags belonged to her."

"They bought the story about the funeral?" Babá asked.

"Yep," Hector said.

"What about *our* suitcase?" Mamá pointed to the shabby, old-fashioned case leaning against the wall in the hall.

Hector turned to face her. "You only have the one?"

Mamá blushed. "Aye, yes. Just one."

"I'll text my mom and tell her to come up and pretend it's another one of hers," Gertie said.

"No one would believe this is Diane's," Mamá said.

"It's okay. I'll take it down to her," Hector offered.

Gertie filled with anxiety as Hector took the suitcase and headed back down the stairs. What if the other demigods didn't buy it?

"Okay," Babá said. "It's time to put on a show. Is everyone ready?"

"What is the show again?" Phoebe asked.

"We are pretending to go to Klaus's funeral," Babá explained. "Just pretend to be in mourning."

"It won't be hard to act like I'm sad," Nikita said. "I'm so scared, that my eyes keep filling up with tears. Making myself cry will be a piece of cake."

"And once we are in New York, that is what we shall have!" Babá exclaimed. "A piece of cake. I will bake my best one yet!"

He pinched Phoebe's cheek and patted Gertie's head. Then he poked Nikita's belly and made her smile.

He was such a clown, but Gertie was grateful for him.

Jeno turned to Gertie. "We should fly to the hearse *now*, while Hector is speaking with the demigods at the taxi."

"Right now?" she asked, not looking forward to the piercing sun and to the risk to Jeno's nearly drained body.

He nodded.

Mamá hugged Gertie. "Be careful. Both of you."

Jeno telepathically asked Diane to have the driver open the back of the hearse. Once he received confirmation that the hearse door was open, Jeno took Gertie's hand, and together they flew like speeding bullets directly for the coffin. She flew on Jeno's back between him and the sun, shielding him with her body. The sun seemed to sear her flesh, and they had a clunky, awkward landing after she snapped open the lid of the coffin and pulled it closed again.

"Are you okay?" she asked Jeno.

Jeno turned on his side and slipped an arm beneath her neck, trying to make them both comfortable in the small space. "Yes. All in one piece, I think. And it smells good in here."

"Nice and new," she agreed, recovering from her stinging flesh.

They both laughed. They were so nervous and frightened, that they were laughing and crying at the same time.

"I was so worried," she whispered, even though she knew she didn't have to. She could communicate with him telepathically, but talking brought her comfort. "I couldn't stand the thought of what happened to Calandra happening to you." She clutched the locket at her throat.

He stroked her cheek with his other hand. His mind was blocked, though.

"What are you thinking that you have to keep me out of it?" she asked.

He let down the guard.

My consolation was that if the sun destroyed me, then at least you would have your humanity back.

Gertie shivered. "Don't talk like that."

"I didn't say anything."

She smiled and punched him. "I meant, don't *think* like that."

He kissed her cheek. "This trip will be so much better with you here with me."

"Just like old times," she said.

"Not so old, but yes." He gave her a smile that seemed partly sad, but his guard went up again.

She didn't ask what he was thinking. She already knew. He was thinking that she was with him only because she hadn't become human again. If she had, she would be with Hector.

She blocked her mind as she admitted to herself that it was true. She loved Jeno, and she would find a way to be happy with him when the war was over, but part of her heart would always belong to Hector.

"Listen," Jeno said. "They are loading Klaus's coffin."

Gertie reached out and sensed the other coffin slide into place beside theirs in the back of the hearse.

"That was quick," she whispered.

"Gertie, is that you?" Klaus asked in a whispered voice from inside his tomb.

"Klaus? Are you okay?" she whispered back.

"As well as can be expected, but I've never been so thirsty in my life."

CHAPTER FIVE

New York

Gertie was distraught by the way their coffin was tossed about by the men loading the cargo into the belly of the plane. She and Jeno bumped their heads and knees repeatedly and were thankful when the box stopped moving and they seemed to be in their final position for the flight. Klaus wasn't beside them, like he'd been in the hearse, but he wasn't so far away that she couldn't hear him.

"Someone should give those guys a raise," Klaus said, once the noise had settled down. "They put a lot of effort into their jobs."

Gertie giggled. "I wonder how they'd react if we popped open our lids to complain."

Then she remembered that Klaus's lid was chained closed. And then she remembered about the key. Who had it?

Jeno told her telepathically that Hector had given it to her mother.

Why my mother?

He was afraid Nico or Marta wouldn't be able to resist opening it.

"Hector's not on the plane," she said out loud. "He's not going to make it, is he?"

She'd had a feeling this would happen. Hector had been afraid that if either of the demigods had followed him to the supposed funeral, everyone else would be in danger of missing the flight. He had stayed behind to distract the guards.

"I'll go back for him tonight," Jeno said. "Try not to worry. Unlike mine, his own people won't try to kill him."

"You two planned this all along, didn't you?" she accused.

"We have to be there to fight Euripides," he said. "I only came along to make sure *you* did."

"Well, I'm following you back tonight."

"No, you aren't. You have to stay for Klaus."

"I think that's a good idea, Gertie," Klaus said. "I'm going to need your expertise."

Gertie laughed. "My expertise? I'm afraid I don't have much."

"I'll help you feed before I leave," Jeno said. "Both of you."

"What a treat," Klaus said. "I can't wait."

"I bet you never imagined your first flight abroad would be quite like this," Gertie teased.

"It's not every day a passenger is given his very own bunk to lie down in," Klaus said with a laugh. "I know that much."

"Ours is probably more comfortable," Gertie said. "It's newer and has a soft pillow."

"Yeah, I don't have a pillow."

"I'd rather be in Klaus's," Jeno said. "I don't like the way this silk is sticking to my skin."

"I personally prefer these splinters," Klaus said, and they all laughed.

Joking back and forth made the flight tolerable, as did checking on the minds of the Angelis family flying for the first time. Babá was especially entertaining, because every time the plane jerked with the turbulence, he cried out, "Thee moy!" And each time, Gertie, Jeno, and Klaus would break out into another round of giggles.

Gertie tried throughout the flight to reach out to Hector, but she was unable to make contact with him. She hoped and prayed he was okay. She prayed to Hephaestus to watch over him.

Eight hours later, after the plane had already come to a stop and they'd been waiting to be unloaded for what seemed like an eternity, Klaus said, "By the way, Jeno. I'm sorry I tried to kill you earlier today. That wasn't me, man."

"I know," Jeno said. "You will probably try it again, but I won't hold it against you."

They giggled once more and then were relieved to sense the workers unloading the cargo. They braced themselves for the bumpy ride. Klaus cried out when he hit his head, and for a few moments, they all worried he'd been heard. Luckily, no one could pry his coffin open, even if they wanted to.

It took an hour for the funeral people to load them into a hearse, and then another hour for them to arrive on Staten Island at Gertie's house. Once their coffins had been set down in the living room, and the two men from the funeral home had left with a generous payment, Gertie and Jeno pushed open the lid and jumped out.

"What about me?" Klaus asked.

Gertie asked Jeno telepathically if he thought it was safe to let Klaus out.

Jeno frowned. "We'll take a chance when we feed. Then we'll put him back in for safe keeping."

Gertie noticed the faces of the humans go pale.

Even Nikita kept her distance.

Babá changed the subject by complimenting the house, over and over—every little thing: the size of the rooms, the number of rooms, the crystal chandeliers, the grand piano, the crown molding, the paintings on the walls, and the vases and other décor Diane's decorator had chosen and carefully placed around the rooms. He held nothing back.

Mamá, on the other hand, was struggling with her feelings of jealousy over her friend's luxurious lifestyle, and she also felt overwhelmed by the grandeur, even sick to her stomach. It was too much for her to take in, so she focused on the piano. "Do you play, Diane?"

"Oh, no. I never cared to learn."

"Your husband, then?"

Diane laughed. "You must be kidding. None of us play, not even Gertie, but the piano plays on its own. I'll show you."

Gertie wished her mother had a clue about how Mamá was feeling.

Even Nikita and Phoebe were speechless. Nikita felt like Mamá—overwhelmed. Phoebe was in awe and trying to soak up the details, like Babá, except without the boisterous commentary.

"I wonder how you water those plants?" Babá pointed to the greenery hanging along the top of an arch separating the living room from the foyer. "It's so high up. You must need a ladder."

"I have plant people," Diane said without hesitating. "They come once a week."

"Do they take care of the outdoor gardens, too, then?" Babá asked.

"Oh, no." Diane laughed. "The gardeners do that. And they come daily, since the grounds are quite large."

Gertie sensed Mamá was on the verge of fainting.

"Why don't I show everyone where the guest rooms are?" Gertie suggested to her mother. "So they can unpack and make themselves comfortable?"

"I'd love to make myself comfortable," Klaus said from his tomb, though no one but Gertie and Jeno could hear him through the thick wood. "Any day now."

Be patient, Jeno said to him telepathically just as Diane was saying, "That's a good idea, Gertie."

Then Gertie read Klaus's self-deprecating thoughts. He was thinking that his baby brother had been stuck in his coffin for three years. Klaus berated himself for not being able to tolerate a single day.

Don't be so hard on yourself, Jeno said to him.

Gertie added, *I'll show everyone to their rooms and then we'll help you out, okay?*

"Sure, man."

Gertie led their guests upstairs past her bedroom, bath, sitting area, entertainment room, and library. She took her friends to the two guest rooms that shared a Jack and Jill bath on the opposite side of her entertainment room. It was where her overnight guests were meant to sleep, but Gertie could count on one hand the number of times she'd had sleepovers.

Beyond the two guest rooms was another suite, nearly as large as Gertie's. It was where Gertie's grandmother had lived up until she died—not quite a year ago. Gertie's stomach tightened into a knot as memories of her grandmother swept over her. She'd been the only person who'd seemed to really care about Gertie—that is, before Gertie had gone to Athens. (Gertie would be forever grateful to Jeno, Hector, Nikita, and the rest of the Angelis family for picking up where her grandmother had left off—for making Gertie feel loved.)

She supposed Mamá and Babá could take that room, if they preferred. She decided to let them choose.

As she had expected, they preferred the smaller rooms and the Jack and Jill bath, which was good, because Gertie noticed that her grandmother's things hadn't been removed from the suite.

Gertie wondered if her parents ever planned to go through any of her grandmother's possessions.

Probably not. Her parents never came upstairs. Ever.

There was a third floor where the cook and housekeeper used to live until the cook got married and the housekeeper got pregnant within six months of one another. They had both moved out and now commuted each day.

Gertie decided not to share the details about the staff and their old rooms with the Angelis family.

"I hope you don't mind sleeping in the queen bed with Phoebe," Gertie said to Nikita when they were left alone in one of the guest rooms. Each had a single queen-sized bed.

Nikita unloaded the pile of clothing Mamá had given her onto the bed. "I wouldn't mind, but Mamá and Babá want her to sleep in their room, on the chaise."

"Why? That's silly."

"They wanted me to sleep in there, too, but I told them no way. This is probably the only time in my life that I'll have a room to myself."

"Oh, don't say that."

"Well, it's true."

"You can hang those up in that closet, if you want," Gertie said. "Or those drawers in that chest are empty, too."

"Thanks."

Her mom called up to her from downstairs.

Gertie went to the balcony overlooking the first-floor living room and peered at her mother from the balustrade.

"What about Jeno? Are you going to put him on the third floor?" her mother asked.

Jeno quickly told Gertie telepathically not to tell the others about his and Hector's plan to fight in Athens.

"Um, I guess so," Gertie said to her mother. "He and Hector can share Connie's old room." Connie was the cook.

We need to feed as soon as possible, Jeno added.

Gertie descended the stairs. "First, we need to go out with Klaus for a while. Don't wait up."

Her mother opened her mouth as if to say something, but then shut it again.

As they flew across the night sky above New York City, Gertie and Jeno each held one of Klaus's arms. Jeno didn't seem to think that Euripides could control Klaus from this distance, but he didn't want to take any chances.

"Where are we going?" Klaus asked.

"To a pub I know," Jeno said.

"What?" Gertie was shocked. "You know of a pub here, in New York City?"

Jeno rolled his eyes. "You forget how old I am. Don't you think I'd have traveled the world over several times by now?"

"Have you?" Klaus asked.

"No," Jeno admitted. "But I've been to this city many times—just not in recent years."

"How long has it been?" Gertie asked.

Jeno cocked his head to one side. "Thirty or forty years, maybe."

"Then that pub is probably long gone," Gertie said.

"Not this one," Jeno said enigmatically.

He led them into a dark alley near a busy street, and then together they took to the sidewalk among the mortals. Gertie smelled the warm, sweet blood of every person within a mile radius of her. It made her even more desperate to drink.

They stopped in front of a very old inn. The cracked wooden sign above the door read, "The Vulture."

Gertie narrowed her eyes. "What are you not telling me, Jeno? Are there vampires in America, too? In *this city*? Is this another Hotel Frangelico?"

"Not exactly," Jeno said.

"Jeno, what's going on?" Klaus asked.

"Come inside," he said. "You'll see."

They entered a lobby that was dark and dusty. An old chandelier hung above them, and there was a mirror on one wall which, of course, did not reflect their images as they passed a grouping of leather chairs. The music from the pub, and some of the colorful lights, poured into the otherwise unremarkable room. Behind the counter sat a beautiful young woman, not much older than Gertie.

"Passphrase, please," she said, without looking up.

"All is fair in love and war," Jeno said.

"Thank you," she said, again without looking up. "You may enter."

CHAPTER SIX

The Vulture

I need to warn you," Jeno said to Gertie and Klaus in the lobby of the old inn. "This pub will test us before allowing us all the way inside."

"Test us?" Klaus repeated. "In what way?"

"It wants to make sure we're worthy." Jeno lifted a finger. "Just follow my lead and stay close. We might not make it, but, if we do, we won't have to hunt tonight."

Klaus frowned in a way that reminded Gertie of Babá. "I don't like the sound of this."

Jeno put a hand on each of the other's shoulders. "The answer to the question is *love*." He gave their shoulders a squeeze. "Don't be afraid."

Gertie narrowed her eyes as Jeno turned his back on her and walked through a door. When she tried to follow, she felt herself entering a strange purple substance that felt a lot like hair gel. She closed her eyes and rubbed her face. Her skin felt normal. The substance was an illusion.

"Jeno?" she called.

He didn't answer. When she opened her eyes, she found herself alone in a small, dark room. The purple substance had disappeared. She looked back for a door but found only a blank brown wall. Where were Jeno and Klaus? Her throat tightened with fear.

In front of her was a rectangular chest, and on top of it was an open book with a quill in an ink jar beside it. She peered at the musty pages of the book and read:

What is the greatest virtue?

Jeno had given her the answer, even though, now that she knew the question, she had to admit she didn't agree with it. Still, she took up the quill and set out to write "love." What came from the tip of the trembling quill was the answer in her head: "wisdom."

The floor dropped from beneath her and she cried out as she fell at least fifteen feet before landing in a big gooey mess. It was a pit of black, oily tar. She was covered in it from her neck down, and it reeked like burnt rubber.

Gross.

And Jeno and Klaus were still nowhere in sight.

Across from her was another door with a sign above it that read, "Only one may pass." As she struggled with the thick tar on her way to the door, Klaus dropped through the ceiling and landed a few feet away, splashing the gunk in her hair.

"This is disgusting," he said.

"What happened to you? Where were you?" she asked.

"In a little dark room. There was this chest and a book with a question."

"I was there, too. What did you write as your answer?"

"I tried to write *love*," he said. "But the quill wouldn't cooperate."

"Same here. I wrote *wisdom*."

"*Honesty*," Klaus said.

"How can *love* be the best answer?" she complained as she crawled through the tar pit toward the door.

She supposed it depended on who was asking the question.

Klaus followed her, pushing his way through the black, oily slime, and then they helped one another to their feet.

"Only one may pass," Klaus read out loud.

"You go," Gertie said. "You need to feed more than I do. I'll wait here. Tell Jeno to come back for me. Then hopefully we can have a shower."

"Are you kidding? I'm not leaving you behind. What if Jeno and I can't make it back?"

Suddenly the floor lifted up, like an elevator, and Gertie felt herself moving through the purple gel and back into the dark room with the book. Klaus was beside her. They were both clean of the tar, and the illusion of gel had disappeared.

"Whoa. This is the strangest pub I've ever been to," Klaus said.

"Isn't this the *only* pub you've ever been to?"

"True, that," he admitted with a sheepish grin.

Gertie peered at the open book. The question (*What is the greatest virtue?*) remained on the page, but no answer followed. She took up the quill and wrote "love." It occurred to her that whoever was orchestrating the illusion felt satisfied to have taught her a lesson. Her love for Klaus as a friend and his for her when they had each refused to leave the other behind must have given them this second chance. She handed the quill over to Klaus.

He dipped the tip in the ink jar, and, as he wrote "love," he said, "But keep in mind that with true love, there must be honesty. They go hand in hand."

"Who are you talking to?" Gertie asked.

"The pub, or whoever or *whatever* is judging us." He returned the quill to the jar.

"Now what do we do?" she asked.

Klaus shrugged. "Maybe we go through that door."

"Isn't that the door we came in?"

Klaus shrugged again but cautiously led the way. He pushed open the creaky door, took a deep breath, and looked back at her before stepping through. Gertie followed, expecting purple hair gel, but instead, was greeted with bright light—not the kind that hurt. Inside was a large pool shaped like a clam shell with a glowing white swan floating on the surface of the clear, glassy water.

The swan's beak moved, and from it came a woman's voice. "If you could say anything to the goddess of love, what would it be?"

"I would tell her she was beautiful," Klaus said. "Because it would be the truth."

Klaus was lifted into the air, where he disappeared.

"Klaus!" Gertie cried.

"And you?" the swan asked.

Gertie frowned. "I'd ask a question," she said truthfully.

The swan stretched her neck and peered more closely at Gertie, scrutinizing her. "What question?"

Oh, why hadn't she just said the same thing as Klaus?

Gertie could think of plenty of questions, though, for the goddess of love, and, after a moment, settled on the most important one. "Why don't my parents love me?"

"Because you don't belong to them," the swan replied. "You never belonged to them."

A lump rose in Gertie's throat, and she wished she hadn't asked. What had she expected to hear? She'd been hoping to hear that they *did* love her but that they just didn't know how to show it.

My parents don't love me, she thought to herself. *They don't even know me, really. My grandmother was the only person who ever knew the real Gertie. Even Mamá and Babá, as kind as they are and as much as I love them, don't know the real me through and through like my grandmother did.*

"Your grandmother isn't dead," the swan said.

Gertie's mouth dropped open.

"She's among the gods."

"In the Underworld?" Gertie asked.

"Ask your other question," the swan said. "The one about the boy."

Gertie's face burned in spite of her low blood supply. She looked at the marble floor.

"Go on," the swan demanded. "Ask."

"What should I do about Hector?"

"Never give up on love," the swan replied.

Gertie suddenly recalled that the swan was one of Aphrodite's sacred animals. Was this the actual goddess of love? In New York City? "Are you..."

"You have a loving heart," the swan interrupted. "But to enter this house, you must also have a fighting spirit. Good luck, young demigod."

In the next instant, Gertie found herself in another room as large as an indoor stadium. Jeno and Klaus both slammed swords against the weapons of two enormous girl warriors. Before Gertie could cross the room to help her friends, another female warrior charged her.

A sword appeared at Gertie's feet, so she swept it up and swung it at her attacker, but the warrior easily knocked it from her hands. Gertie then relied on her vampire speed and endurance to dodge the attacker's sword as it sliced through the air toward her repeatedly.

"I thought you'd never get here!" Jeno cried from across the large room, as he continued to fight with his opponent. "How hard is it to write a one-word answer?"

"A lot harder than you think!" Klaus replied just before the girl warrior kicked him to the ground. "Why didn't you tell us about this part? This can't be better than hunting." He scrambled to his feet.

"Consider this training!" Jeno shouted without missing a beat in his fight. "You may need to help fight against Euripides!"

"If I survive this!" Klaus yelled out as he dodged the sword cutting through the air at him. In another moment, his weapon clattered across the marble floor, and, like Gertie, he was left to dodge and duck.

The blood of the warriors smelled amazing to Gertie, and, without meaning to, she opened her mouth with fangs extended. Telepathically, she asked Jeno if the warriors were demigods.

"Yes," he said as he crashed his weapon against that of his opponent. "Amazons. Daughters of Ares. If we win, we get to drink."

"Ares won't come after us for that?" she asked.

"Not as long as we stop at one pint," he said.

This good news gave Gertie and Klaus the edge they needed to scramble for their swords and fight. No more ducking. No more dodging. They slammed their swords against the armor of their opponents, trying every which way to disarm them.

It only took Gertie a few more minutes to overwhelm the Amazon warrior fighting her. As soon as the girl's sword crashed to the floor, Gertie was at her throat faster than the eye can blink. She paralyzed her victim and drank a full pint before heaving the girl aside. Gertie wiped the excess from her lips and noticed the other two had also taken their attackers, but Klaus didn't seem to know he was supposed to stop. Gertie could tell by the coloring of his victim that he had gone too far.

She and Jeno pulled Klaus away from the girl, who slumped, nearly unconscious, on the floor.

When Klaus met Gertie's eyes, she realized he was possessed by Euripides. The evil, maniacal expression was one that her sweet friend could never pull off on his own. A chill ran down her spine as she was reminded of the expression on Damien's face when he clung to the back of Vladimir.

Jeno realized it, too. "We need to get him out of here! Come on!"

There was only one way out. Gertie held one of Klaus's arms as Jeno held the other, and together they entered the smoky bar.

A large, well-built man turned from where he'd been playing billiards and glared at them. Gertie realized he couldn't be a man. He must be a god.

That's Ares, Jeno warned her telepathically. *He's not very happy about what just happened.*

Longish red hair fell to the god's shoulders, and blazing blue eyes narrowed at her. He had a square jaw with a five-o'clock shadow and a cleft in his chin. His biceps were nearly the width of her torso. And he looked ready to attack.

"It wasn't Klaus," Gertie blurted out. "He's possessed. We need to get him out of here."

"Or drive a billiards stick through his heart," Ares said. "Before he hurts someone else."

"Please, Lord Ares," Jeno said. "We intend to destroy the one responsible for this. He's raging war tonight in Athens. Let us pass."

"You are heading into war now?" Ares asked with a look of lust on his face.

Jeno struggled with his grip on Klaus. "After we return our friend to his chains."

Ares lifted his chin and rested his hands on his narrow hips. "You plan to fight against your own people?"

"Just one vampire and his clan," Jeno replied.

Klaus struggled hard against Jeno and Gertie.

"And then we plan to fight *with* the vampires," Gertie added.

Klaus turned and glared at her before sinking his fangs into her wrist and taking some of her newly consumed blood. She pulled her arm away, and Klaus broke free of Jeno.

The other men and women in the room—there were maybe ten of them—jumped from their chairs and barstools, bracing themselves against the enraged and loose vampire. Gertie and Jeno flew around, chasing him, knocking over tables and chairs and crashing into mirrored walls that did not reflect them, but they couldn't stop Klaus from ripping through the flesh of several people with his fangs before grabbing hold of a pool stick and launching it toward Jeno, who barely dodged it in time.

Gertie had a horrible feeling in the pit of her stomach when Ares leapt from the floor and slammed himself into Klaus, mid-flight. Stunned, Klaus fell against a wall, taking down a table full of drinks and food with him.

The violent hit seemed to have momentarily freed him from the power of Euripides. Klaus returned Gertie's terrified gaze with his own.

He looked about to say something—maybe an apology—when another billiards stick flew through the air from the fist of Ares and lodged into Klaus's chest.

The look of utter surprise that crossed Klaus's face broke Gertie's heart.

"No!" she screamed.

CHAPTER SEVEN

The Messenger and the God of Light

D o something!” Gertie cried as Klaus stared back at her with a look of shock on his face.

Blood soaked into his shirt around the pole sticking out of his chest. He gasped and tried to speak but failed.

A bright light flickered into the room, and with her acute vampire senses, Gertie recognized the swan flapping her glorious luminous wings before landing beside Ares and the pool table. When she settled beside him, she transformed from the bird into the most beautiful woman Gertie had ever seen. She had strawberry blonde curls held back from her greenish-blue eyes by a golden clamshell comb. Her full lips were turned down into a frown as she faced Ares and said, “What have you done?”

“He was a danger to everyone here,” Ares growled.

“This thin, fragile creature was a threat to *you*?” she challenged.

“He was possessed by a demon,” Ares explained.

“Not a demon,” Gertie couldn’t resist blurting out. Who did she think she was, correcting the god of war? “A vampire.”

Ares scowled at her. To the ten or so onlookers, Ares commanded, “Leave us.”

The patrons of The Vulture quickly filed from the room. Even the bartender, cook, and waitress left.

"There's no demon in him now," Aphrodite pointed out as the people were leaving. "He's a loving soul who doesn't deserve this death."

"What would you have me do?" Ares said in a tone of complaint.

"Call Hermes. Doesn't he owe you a favor?"

"Actually, I owe him."

"Then call him and owe him another. Tell him to find Apollo."

Gertie and Jeno had rushed to Klaus's side. Gertie wanted to dislodge the billiards stick, but Jeno had told her telepathically that Klaus would lose blood more quickly if she did. So, instead, she held the long end of it up, hoping to make Klaus more comfortable, even though Jeno said he was in shock and couldn't feel anything.

Jeno helped her hold the stick, because he knew it made her feel better.

This doesn't look good, he warned her. *Prepare yourself to say goodbye.*

Aphrodite is helping him, she insisted. *And what could I possibly say to Mamá and Babá?* The thought of Nikita and Phoebe's pain made Gertie nauseous.

Fortunately the stick didn't go through his heart. If it had...

Please help him, Gertie prayed to Aphrodite and Ares.

Gertie hadn't yet finished her prayer when a large black rabbit landed among them and then instantly transformed into a bearded man with dark hair and dark eyes. He held the caduceus, which told Gertie right away who he was, because she had read about him in her books.

She gawked at Hermes as the other gods asked him to find Apollo as soon as possible.

I'm surprised he's still alive, Jeno said when Hermes had vanished as quickly as he had appeared. *Aphrodite must be helping him.*

Gertie continued to pray to the gods of love and war as they waited anxiously for Hermes to return with Apollo. After a few moments, Klaus closed his eyes and hung his head. He didn't seem to be breathing.

"Is he…?" Gertie couldn't finish her sentence.

"Not yet," Jeno said, glancing at Aphrodite. His thoughts revealed that he suspected the goddess of interfering with the arrival of Thanatos, the god of death.

In another moment, a golden wolf, the size of the pool table, bounded into the pub, followed by the black rabbit. As soon as they had landed, they transformed into men. Both wore grave expressions.

The fair-skinned Apollo, with golden hair and bright blue eyes, shifted his quiver of silver arrows aside as he looked upon the limp body belonging to Klaus.

"He's one of mine," Apollo said.

"He's a demigod?" Gertie asked in shock. Being a son to Apollo would explain Klaus's inability to tell a lie. It would also explain why he and Nikita had such beautiful singing voices.

"Not demigod, but down the line," Apollo said. "Even so, I'm sorry to say I'm too late."

"But you haven't even tried to help him!" Gertie shouted.

Watch yourself, Jeno warned.

"There's nothing I can do," Apollo said kindly. "We're out of time."

Just then, a young god, about Gertie's own age, appeared beside Klaus. She recognized him from Charon's raft. He was Thanatos, the god of death.

"Please!" she begged him. "Don't take him!"

The young god frowned as he lifted the transparent soul of Klaus from the limp body. In a moment, they were gone, and Klaus's body was cold to the touch.

Jeno put his arms around Gertie and whispered, "I'm so sorry. I wish I wouldn't have brought us here."

"This isn't your fault."

Gertie turned to the gods still present in the room, her memory of one of the ancient myths on her tongue. "Orpheus went to Hades once and…"

"So?" Apollo asked.

"Do you think it's possible..." she dropped off as the tears overwhelmed her and she could no longer speak. Poor Klaus! And what would she say to his family! She wished she could die, too.

Don't think like that, Jeno said.

"Can you sing or play a musical instrument?" Apollo asked.

Gertie shook her head.

"But we know someone who can," Jeno said. "He's one of your descendants."

Hector! Gertie thought, and Jeno nodded.

Hermes shook his head at Apollo. "Why are you giving them false hope?"

"You forget who I am," Apollo said.

Gertie's eyes widened. Apollo was also the god of prophecy. "Do you see something?"

"Not clearly," he said.

She wished she had some wine. Maybe then *she* could see the future. "What do you see?"

"It's quite vague, but I see you standing beside Hades."

"Me?" Gertie's mouth hung open.

"If you're going to try to save him, you need to go immediately," Ares said. "There's no time to lose."

"Well, lookie there," Aphrodite said, smiling at Ares. "You do have a heart in there after all." She pressed her palm against his silver armor at his chest.

Ares grinned, but Hermes rolled his eyes. Gertie was so pleased at the hope of saving Klaus that she smiled, too.

Apollo opened his hand, and his lyre appeared. "Have Hector play on this." He handed the instrument to Gertie. "However, there are no guarantees when dealing with the lord of the Underworld. Remember that."

Just then, the gods and the pub faded away, and Gertie was left in a dark alley in Times Square with Jeno at her side, the limp body of Klaus at her feet, and Apollo's golden lyre in her hand.

CHAPTER EIGHT

Emergency Flight to Athens

As quietly as they could, Gertie and Jeno carried the dead body of their friend into the Morgan mansion to the living room, where the old coffin was still lying on the floor. With the utmost care, they laid Klaus into it and closed the lid. Gertie couldn't hold back her tears as they padlocked the chains. They didn't want the others to suspect what had happened. Gertie hid the key in the bottom drawer of the living room armoire, so no one would open it and discover their secret.

Then she broke down into an all out sob fest, clutching Apollo's lyre to her chest.

Jeno took her in his arms and kissed her hair. "We need to go to Athens."

That's when they both sensed the presence of two others awake and nearby. Above them was Nikita looking down from the balcony, white and clinging to the balustrade. A check of her mind revealed she had seen them carry in Klaus. She was in shock, still trying to process what she had witnessed.

Before Gertie or Jeno could reach out to Nikita, to attempt to erase her mind using eye contact, the other person they had sensed entered the room from the hallway. It was Diane.

"Gertie, there you are," Diane said. "I've been waiting up for you."

"Why?" Gertie asked, unused to this kind of attention from the woman.

Diane glanced at Jeno before saying, "I was hoping we could finally have that talk."

As anxious as Gertie was to hear what her mother had to say, she had no choice but to get Hector and take him with her and Jeno to the Underworld as soon as possible. It was their only chance of saving Klaus.

"I'm exhausted," Gertie said. "And I've been through so much lately. Do you mind if we talk tomorrow?"

Diane folded her arms across her chest and glanced again at Jeno. "You aren't planning to sneak off to Athens, are you?"

Now it was Gertie's turn to glance at Jeno, but he offered her no answers. "No. I'm going to bed. Come on, Jeno. I'll show you to your room."

As Gertie clutched Apollo's lyre and made her way to the winding stairs, her mother said, "Sleep well, then. We'll talk tomorrow."

Aren't you going to tell her goodnight or sweet dreams? Jeno asked her telepathically.

That would be awkward.

She picked up on a flurry of his thoughts before he blocked her out. He'd been thinking how sad her relationship was with her mother. He had loved his, and in spite of her becoming a monster, he held onto the old memories of her. He was fond of them and couldn't imagine not having them. Even the memories of his father, before everything had happened, before Jeno had had to kill Vladimir, brought him comfort. He'd loved both his parents, and Gertie didn't seem to know what that was like. Before Jeno had blocked her, Gertie had caught him wondering if she even knew what love was.

She didn't respond to his thoughts, since he had tried to block them and hadn't meant for her to hear them. But she wanted to tell him that she did know what love was. She had loved her grandmother. And she loved the Angelis family. And she loved Jeno, too.

And Hector, Jeno added.

Yes, she admitted after a few moments, when she realized her attempt to block him had failed. She hoped and prayed Hector was okay and hated that she hadn't been able to sense him since leaving Athens. *And Hector.*

And she felt something for her parents, too, but it was an awkward, disappointed, guarded kind of thing that she didn't want to think about for too long.

When they reached the second floor, Nikita stood, white as a ghost, waiting for them.

"What happened to Klaus?" she asked. "Is he...," she swallowed hard, "dead?"

"What?" Gertie walked past and started for the third level. "Don't be ridiculous. Don't you think I'd tell you if something that terrible had happened to your brother?"

Jeno said nothing as he followed Gertie up the stairs.

Nikita was right on his heels. "I know what I saw."

"We mesmerized him, so he'd be easier to handle," Gertie lied. "It's a vampire thing. Don't worry about it. You wouldn't understand."

"I saw the blood on his shirt," Nikita insisted.

"The blood was someone else's," Gertie said. "He's still learning to feed. You should see how messy he is." She forced a laugh. "Isn't he messy, Jeno?"

Jeno made no reply.

Help me out, she said to him telepathically.

She already knows the truth.

When they reached the third floor, Nikita said, "Stop lying to me. Tell me the truth. Is he dead?"

"Lower your voice," Gertie whispered. "You're going to wake up the whole house."

"It's true, isn't it, Jeno?" Nikita asked, bursting into tears. "My brother's dead. Now both of them are gone. Damien and Klaus."

Seeing her best friend's pain brought another wave of tears to Gertie's eyes. "We're trying to save Klaus. We might be able to bring him back."

Nikita covered her face. "So it's true. He really is dead?"

Jeno nodded, explaining what had happened back at The Vulture. "We hope it's only temporary. We're going tonight to get Hector to go with us to the Underworld."

Gertie squeezed Nikita's hand. "Apollo gave us his lyre for Hector. We're hoping Hector's singing can move the gods of the Underworld, like Orpheus did."

Nikita's eyes grew wide. Then she clenched her fists at her sides and said, "Take me with you."

"It's much too dangerous for a mortal," Jeno said.

Gertie put her hands on her dear friend's shoulders. "We promise to do everything we can. I'll even offer to trade places with him. Believe me, Nikita. I'd rather be dead than see you and your family suffer any more pain because of me."

"Why do you think this is your fault?" Nikita asked. "Did you kill my brother?"

Gertie took a step back, her jaw falling open. "No. No, I didn't. But…"

"Then this is not your fault," Nikita said. "All of this with the demigods and the vampires—this was all a problem long before you came to Athens."

Gertie's heart filled with even more love for her friend. She was grateful that Nikita didn't blame her.

"But if you don't take me with you," Nikita added, "I'm telling my parents the truth about Klaus."

Gertie's mouth fell open again. "What? Nikita, please."

"I'm serious," she said. "You aren't the only one who would do anything to bring Klaus back. You're taking me with you, and that's the end of the discussion. Now, bite me, so I can fly and have superpowers, too."

Gertie and Jeno exchanged glances.

"Don't look at me," Jeno said. "She's *your* friend."

"I didn't know a vampire had to be asked more than once to drink," Nikita said to Jeno with a huff. "Is there something wrong with my blood?"

"Not at all, miss. But I would never want your mother on my bad side," Jeno said. "She's more likely to forgive Gertie than me."

"My mother never has to know," Nikita said.

"Never has to know what?" Mamá asked from the bottom of the stairs on the second floor. "What's going on up there?"

Gertie wanted to disappear. Since she was a vampire, she literally could, but it wouldn't solve their problem.

Jeno was on it, however. He trained his eyes on Mamá, mesmerizing her. "You look sleepy, Marta. Why don't you go back to bed?"

Her eyes locked onto his. Slowly, she nodded. "I am very sleepy. Yes, I think I will go back to bed. Good night."

I can't believe that worked, Jeno said telepathically to Gertie. *She's usually on her guard against me.*

Nikita looked horrified as she watched her mother turn, like a zombie, away from them and head toward the guest room. But, once Mamá had disappeared behind the bedroom door, Nikita turned to Gertie and said, "Do it now."

Gertie glanced over the balustrade, making sure no one else was up in the Morgan mansion.

"In here," she said, leading the others into the room that belonged to Connie, the cook. The woman no longer spent her nights there, but the room still held many of her things. Connie used the room to nap in the afternoon after lunch sometimes—or at least she had while Gertie was at home six months ago.

Gertie had forgotten about the clock collection in Connie's room, but was reminded again when she saw it from Jeno's appreciative eyes. He entered the room and was immediately drawn to the dozen cuckoo clocks on the wall and to the antique clocks on the built-in bookcase.

"Let's get this over with," Nikita said. "What do you want? My wrist? Or my throat?"

Gertie sensed Nikita trembling, and she could hear her friend's heart beating out of control.

"Don't be frightened," Gertie said. "It doesn't hurt. You'll first feel numb and very still, and then dizzy. And then, you'll feel incredibly strong and powerful."

"Okay, just do it." Nikita stretched out her arm and closed her eyes. Her teeth were chattering, and more tears formed around her lashes. She was terrified but wanted to help save her brother.

Gertie felt like a monster as she gingerly took her friend's quivering arm and pierced the wrist with her fangs. She took only enough to make sure the virus would penetrate Nikita's blood system. Then she pressed the wound until the bleeding stopped.

A check of Nikita's mind revealed the various stages Gertie remembered experiencing all too well. Jeno studied the clock collection as Gertie waited for her friend to feel the power.

After a few moments, Nikita's eyes opened wide, and she looked at Gertie with a huge grin. "This is incredible! I feel amazing!"

Gertie and Jeno smiled.

Nikita's eyes got even wider. She was just realizing that she had x-ray vision. Nikita glanced over Jeno's body and blushed bright red.

Gertie and Jeno laughed.

Then Jeno looked at the clocks again and turned back to Gertie with an expression of panic. "We need to go," Jeno said pointing to the clocks. "I forgot about the time difference. It'll be dawn in Athens in less than an hour."

Gertie frowned. Poor Hector. He'd been fighting all night without their help. What if he'd been killed? What if they had to go to the Underworld to save both boys? "Let's go."

Jeno gracefully leapt through the third-floor bedroom window into the cold night sky above Staten Island. Gertie motioned for Nikita to go next, but Nikita looked down at the ground below and shook her head.

Nikita stepped back from the window. "I forgot how afraid I am of heights."

"Then wait for us here," Gertie said as she leapt through the window. "We have to hurry."

"No. I want to help." Trembling, Nikita stepped onto the ledge and clung to the window frame. "Can I ride on your back with my eyes closed?"

Gertie was tempted to just fly away and leave her friend there, where she would be safe; but she knew how Nikita felt. Gertie knew how important it was to Nikita to help her brother.

Gertie backed up to the window. "Climb on."

Nikita wrapped her warms around Gertie's neck and her legs around Gertie's hips.

Then she screamed in Gertie's ear and strangled her all the way to Athens.

CHAPTER NINE

Aftermath

As Gertie and her friends reached Athens in the pre-dawn night, they were alarmed by the rising smoke curling up into the almost invisible clouds of the dark sky. The smoke came from more than one location. Gertie reached out with her mind for Hector but made no contact.

"Oh my gods!" Nikita shouted in Gertie's ear. "Holy tomato! I'm closing my eyes again."

"Can you get a read on Euripides, or any of the other vampires?" Gertie asked Jeno.

"No. Nothing. They must have us blocked." *Either that, or they're dead,* Jeno thought.

Gertie hoped that wasn't the case. As much as she wanted to stop Euripides and his clan, she didn't want all the vampires dead. "What about Hector? I can't sense him, either."

"Neither can I. Let's move closer to the city. Where to? The acropolis?"

"Let's try the Angelis's apartment building first," she suggested. "Maybe Hector is waiting for us there."

As they descended toward the city, Nikita couldn't control her squealing. Gertie was tempted to drop her, because it was annoying and because Gertie was already so stressed out. But, along with Apollo's lyre, she held onto Nikita's legs, wrapped tightly around her hips.

"It's okay," Gertie murmured. "We're almost there."

But Gertie had barely uttered those words when her vampire vision pinpointed what was left of the Angelis apartment building. It was one of the sources of smoke billowing into the sky. Although the flames were out and the smoke was gray instead of black, only half of the building remained. Even the basement was visible from above without the need for x-ray vision. Gertie cringed at the thought of Nikita's reaction and of breaking the news to the rest of her family. All of their treasures, as humble as they might have been, were ruined.

It reminded her of when Athena had destroyed the caves beneath the acropolis and Calandra had tried to save her and her brother's things.

Jeno's expression mirrored hers: utter sadness for the Angelis family.

They landed among the rubble. When Nikita opened her eyes, Gertie closed hers and said, "I'm so sorry."

Nikita said nothing for several minutes. Gertie couldn't get a grasp on the onslaught of thoughts and memories surging through Nikita's mind. It was overwhelming. Gertie opened her eyes to make sure her friend hadn't fainted.

"Nikita?"

With her vampire powers, Nikita climbed up the ruins of the building toward the highest level, hoping to find some remnant of her life. Gertie watched her like a hawk—afraid she would fall or hurt herself in the half-burnt structure barely standing. Aside from the burned kitchen appliances and partial sections of wood and plaster, everything was ash. There was nothing left of Nikita's life among them.

"We have to find Hector," Jeno said, breaking Gertie from her concentration. "Nikita, we need your help. We have to save Klaus, okay?"

Nikita nodded and flew back down, wobbly like a young bird, to the ground level, where they called out for Hector.

Gertie stepped over broken, charred bits of the building, calling out his name, until she nearly tripped over a dead body—or what was left of one. Gertie covered her mouth and gasped when she recognized the woman's face. It was Agatha, one of the demigods who'd been watching the apartment building. And just a few feet away, also dead and partially burned, lay Cadmon.

Gertie wanted to puke.

"Hector?" she screamed as she frantically ran around the rubble, tripping on fallen boards and stepping on broken glass. "Hector, where are you? Can you hear me?"

"Hector!" Nikita shouted, too.

Jeno crouched over another corpse at the back of the basement, where part of the wall was still standing, and a pile of half-burned books lay heaped on the ground. Gertie and Nikita rushed to his side. Gertie could barely breathe.

"Who is it?" Gertie asked, unable to look.

"It's not Hector."

Very little remained of a skeleton among a pile of ash with a golden sword—Hector's sword—lying beside it.

"It could be Euripides," Jeno said. "The shape of the skull reminds me of him."

"Do you think Hector's okay?" Nikita asked.

"I don't know." The first sting of dawn pricked Gertie's skin. "The sun's coming up. What should we do?"

"Let's try Hector's house," Jeno said. "We might make it if we leave now."

Nikita climbed onto Gertie's back once again. Gertie and Jeno darted though the air like two speeding bullets toward the suburban neighborhood where Hector lived. Just as the sun began to really burn, they crashed through an upstairs window and went through the guest bedroom and down the hall directly to Hector's room. They all three landed in a heap on the floor.

"Thank the gods his blinds are closed," Gertie said as she caught her breath.

Nikita lay on the floor beside her, also panting, even though she had only been a passenger.

"I don't sense Hector," Gertie said.

"I really thought he'd be here," Jeno said. "I'm rather worried that he isn't."

"I'm worried, too." Gertie fought tears. Poor Hector. As her skin quickly healed the cuts from the broken window, she prayed to the gods to please let Hector be alive.

Nikita let her tears flow. After seeing her brother dead and her home destroyed, she had nothing left in her to fight.

In the next moment, a voice came from the doorway—a voice without a body. "I *am* here. I'm okay, guys."

Gertie looked toward the doorway in disbelief as Hector became visible. He'd been wearing the helm of invisibility.

"You'll all be glad to know," he said with a smile, "that I've destroyed Euripides and recovered the helm. Not bad, eh?"

The others stared at him in disbelief.

"Aren't you going to say anything?" Hector asked. "Like, *Way to go, Hector.* Or, *You're so awesome, Hector.* Or, *Glad to see you're alive, Hector.*"

Gertie smiled and forgot to block her mind as the desire to kiss him swept over her.

"Glad to see you're alive, Hector," Jeno said, breaking the awkward moment. "We all are."

"I'll bet Klaus will be the gladdest, though." Hector laughed. "No more worry about being possessed and all that."

When Hector noticed the change in the expressions on the faces of his friends, he frowned. "What's happened to Klaus?"

"He was possessed by Euripides again," Gertie said.

Jeno stepped closer to Hector and put a hand on his shoulder. "And Ares... killed him."

"But we're going to get him back," Gertie quickly added. "And you're going to help us."

"Say what?" Hector looked at each of them. "What are you talking about?"

Gertie and Jeno did their best to explain what had happened at The Vulture.

"I can't believe this," Hector said when they had finished. "This sucks so bad. Oh, man."

Nikita broke down in tears.

Hector put an arm around her. "I'm sorry. I'll do what I can to try and get him back. I promise you, okay?"

Nikita nodded.

"The sooner we go the better," Jeno said. "And with the helm, we don't have to wait until dusk."

"I agree we need to go as soon as possible," Hector said. "But I've been waiting for daybreak so I can go back out there without the threat of vampires. I need to go regroup with the other demigods and make sure the bodies of the fallen are recovered."

"Do you really have to do that now?" Gertie asked.

"Cadmon and Agatha died defending me from Euripides," Hector said soberly. "I wouldn't have been able to destroy him without their help. We saved countless lives with that small victory."

"Oh," Gertie said. "I'm sorry. You're right."

"I'm sorry we weren't there fighting alongside you," Jeno said.

"You were exactly where you needed to be," Hector assured him. "But the least I can do is to make sure their bodies are returned to their families."

"Of course," Jeno said. "We will help you."

They decided to take Hector's Mini Cooper. Jeno wore the helm, to render the vehicle and everyone in it invisible.

Hector told them what had happened when Euripides had returned to Athens.

"Where did Euripides get an army of a hundred vampires?" Gertie asked. "I thought he had only twenty or so left in his clan."

"He must have recruited others from surrounding towns and villages," Jeno said.

"That would explain why they struck late instead of right at nightfall," Hector said. "We had begun to believe they weren't coming."

"But when you destroyed Euripides, didn't that wipe out a huge number of them?" Gertie asked.

"Only those in his clan," Jeno said. "And any his clan members might have turned."

Gertie shuddered. Klaus would be back to human form if he hadn't been killed by Ares.

"There were still fifty or sixty swarming through the city." Hector turned into a part of Athens where alarming structural damage had been done. "And there's no telling how many more vampires were made last night, or how many more might be recruited from other areas."

"They're still clearing the roads," Nikita pointed out as they passed a street blocked by fallen rubble.

"The city workers have a lot on their hands today." Hector pulled up to the curb a block away from the Angelis apartment building next to a city truck. "I think this is as close as we can get."

Several workers in hard hats were in the streets clearing fallen debris. Up ahead, near what was left of the Angelis apartment building, an ambulance was parked with its back doors open and its lights casting colors on everything around it.

"Thank the gods," Hector said. "Someone already called for help."

Under the protection of the helm, Gertie, Jeno, and Nikita followed Hector.

Gertie tried not to look as Hector helped the emergency medics place the bodies of Agatha and Cadmon onto stretchers before they were carried to the ambulance. It was traumatic to see, but her eyes were drawn like a magnet.

"It's worse over by the acropolis," one of the medics was saying. "We hauled at least twelve stiffs from the surrounding area."

It's worse than I thought, Jeno said telepathically.

"Don't call them that," Hector said.

"Sorry," the medic turned red. "Did you know these folks?"

"Yes. Their names are Agatha Glavan and Cadmon Lambros." He pulled out his phone. "What hospital are you taking them to? I'll notify their families."

"Evaggelismos General," the other medic said. "And I'm sorry for your loss."

"Do you have any idea what happened last night?" the first medic asked. "The fire chief is spouting spontaneous fires, but it's been too cold for that."

Spontaneous fires? Gertie thought. *Like wildfires? That's ridiculous.*

People will believe the craziest things, Jeno said.

"Vampire attack," Hector said.

"Yeah, right," the first medic shook his head. "I said I was sorry."

Except for the truth, apparently, Gertie thought.

"I'm serious," Hector said. "It's time people stopped pretending they aren't real. They aren't tramps. They're vampires, and they're attacking our city because they've had enough."

Both medics turned white as they closed the doors to their ambulance. They said nothing more to Hector as they climbed inside and drove away.

"Do you think that's the best way?" a red-headed teen asked as he crossed the street toward Hector. "The in-your-face approach?"

Gertie recognized him as the demigod from the emergency council meeting—the one who had stood up for Hector.

"Hey, Lajos," Hector greeted his friend. "Man, I wish I knew. But I think the days of trying to keep it hush-hush might be over."

"I was hoping to find you here," Lajos said.

"Yeah? So glad you made it out alive last night."

"It was worse over by the acropolis. I haven't been to bed yet."

"Me, either."

"With our leadership gone, I was hoping you could tell me where and when we're supposed to meet, to plan for the next attack."

"I don't know, man," Hector glanced back toward the Mini, as though he thought he would see Gertie and the others beneath the helm. Of course, he couldn't. "If you find out, will you call me?"

"My phone's trashed," Lajos said. "That's why I came up here. I lost my dad last night."

"What do you mean, *lost*? Is he…?"

"He's gone, man." Lajos sniffed.

"Oh, no," Hector said. "I'm so sorry."

"I guess you know how it feels," Lajos added.

"Yeah. Yeah, I do."

So many people are losing their parents because of this. Gertie put an arm around Jeno's waist.

"Do you have a place to stay?" Hector asked him. "Any relatives?"

"Up in Patras, I have an aunt," Lajos said. "But I'm not leaving Athens until this conflict is over."

Gertie felt sorry for the boy. She wondered if he had any friends, but her thoughts were soon interrupted when Nikita gasped.

What is it? Gertie asked telepathically, searching her friend's face for clues.

Nikita whispered, "Kiria Petrides, my neighbor. I'm sensing her. She's trapped somewhere!"

Don't speak, Jeno said to Nikita's mind. *I know you're not used to this, but just think what you have to say, so you don't give us away to the others.*

Um, oh gosh, can you hear me? For real? Nikita thought.

Yes. We both can, Gertie said. *You said Mrs. Petrides is trapped? Where?*

I sense her now, too, Jeno said. *Follow my lead. And, Nikita, don't forget, we can't make a sound as long as these city workers are around.*

Got it, Nikita said in her mind. *This is so weird. You really can hear me?*

We really can, Gertie said.

As Hector continued to speak with Lajos about the attack of the previous night, the three teens beneath the helm of Hades made their way toward what was left of the Angelis apartment building. So as to make no noise, they flew—with Jeno in the middle holding each girl's hand. Nikita managed not to squeal as she focused on finding the old woman who was trapped.

She's in here, Jeno said telepathically.

Gertie stared at the half-burned pile of boards in the corner of a room near where all but a ten-foot part of the floor had collapsed. Through the boards, her x-ray vision picked up on the huddled image of old Mrs. Petrides.

"Kiria?" Nikita said. And then she thought, *Oops. I forgot not to speak.*

It's okay, Jeno replied. *Maybe we won't be overheard if we speak softly.*

Gertie's heart pounded in her chest as she looked down to where Hector and Lajos were still talking. She could hear everything acutely, but demigods didn't always have the same talent. Hector had once heard her screams from the acropolis all the way to his house. What if other demigods were around and overheard them beneath the helm? She took a deep breath, trying to calm herself.

This way, Jeno said, leading them behind the piled boards.

Mrs. Petrides was leaning against the last standing wall in the corner on a part of the floor that hadn't fallen. Gertie pushed her hand through Apollo's lyre between the tortoise base and the bottom of the strings and wore it on her arm to free both hands. Then, while Jeno touched their shoulders to keep them protected by the helm, she and Nikita picked up the boards and moved them aside. The old woman was breathing, but her eyes were closed, and she was badly bruised and cut. One of her legs was covered in dried blood.

She's a Halfling, Jeno said.

A what? Gertie doubted he meant the word in the same way Tolkien had used it. Gertie had read everything Tolkien had ever written, including *The Silmarillion*, so she knew Jeno's meaning had to be different.

Could you imagine a Hobbit in Athens? she thought with the briefest of smiles.

A Halfling is someone who's been drained of blood by a vampire but hasn't yet been turned, Jeno explained.

Oh. Gertie and Klaus had both been Halflings. *Is she dying, then?*

I'm afraid so, he said telepathically.

"Kiria?" Nikita repeated. "Can you hear me? It's Nikita Angelis, from upstairs."

The woman blinked several times before opening her eyes and taking in her surroundings with an expression of perplexity. "I don't see you."

"Um, I'm down below. I'll bring help to you. Are you okay?"

"My grandson," she said. "Those devils took my grandson."

Gertie searched the old woman's mind to discover that the vampires had taken her grandson, drained her and left her for dead, and then burned down the building.

"Kiria Petrides, do you mean Phillipos?" Nikita asked.

"Nikita? Is that really you?" the old woman moaned.

"Yes, Kiria." Nikita said. "We're here to help you."

"Forget about *me*," she closed her eyes and struggled to breathe. "I'm an old woman. Help my Phillipos, will you?"

"Yes, Kiria," Nikita said. "I promise. We will find him and make sure he's okay."

What should we do? Gertie asked Jeno. *Are we just going to let her die?*

We have little choice.

Can't she drink my blood? Nikita asked.

It's tainted, Jeno replied.

What about Hector's? Nikita asked. *Couldn't we give her his?*

Jeno frowned. *She'll just be controlled by whoever drained her, just like Klaus was. We have no way of binding her.*

If Euripides turned her... Gertie started to say, but then Jeno interrupted.

She wouldn't be alive if it was Euripides. The only reason she's alive is that she's temporarily animated by the virus from whoever drained her. Her maker is still alive and probably took her grandson to fight with the other vampires. They left her here to die because she's already too old.

She used to babysit me when I was little, Nikita said. *I haven't really talked to her much lately. I should have. She has no one to visit her, except when her grandson comes.*

I'm so sorry, Gertie said. *I wish we could do something, but I agree with Jeno. Turning her seems too dangerous.*

"Kiria Petrides," Nikita said with tears in her eyes. "I will find Phillipos. Okay? Don't you worry. You rest now, okay?"

"Thank you," the old woman said without opening her eyes. "Sweet, Nikita Angelis."

The woman fought hard to breathe. The three teens waited with the woman and watched her take her final breath. Then Nikita gently stretched out her hand and closed the woman's mouth and, full of sadness, the three flew back down to the sidewalk near Hector. He was apparently looking for them as he led Lajos back to the Mini. They were, of course, invisible to him beneath the helm.

"Guys?" Hector said, and probably not for the first time. "Come on, man, answer me. I was just telling Lajos about our quest to the Underworld."

CHAPTER TEN

Flight to Parga

Hector, how could you?" Gertie blurted out. "This was supposed to be a secret mission."

"That is so weird, dude," Lajos said to Hector. "Where is her voice coming from?"

"Like I said, she's under the power of the helm right now."

"That's too cool," he said.

Gertie sucked in air. "You told him about the helm?"

"I really thought you were smarter than this," Jeno said.

"Whoa," Lajos said. "There's another one."

"Can't you erase his memory?" Gertie asked.

"Not while under the protection of the helm," Jeno said.

"Hold up, erase my memory?" Lajos asked. "Are you sure you can trust them, Hector?"

"I'd trust them with my life," he replied.

"I'm not so sure the feeling's mutual," Jeno muttered.

"Look," Hector said. "I know you think I shouldn't have told Lajos, but he can help us."

"How?" Nikita asked.

"There's three of them?" Lajos asked.

"His mother is Alecto, one of the Furies," Hector explained.

Lajos raked his fingers through his vibrant red hair. "There's a place I can go and see her."

"Guys," Hector said. "It's a better way in."

"Don't tell me you're afraid of the Hydra," Gertie challenged.

"You know me better than that," Hector said. "But the acropolis is crawling with people—both tourists and city workers cleaning up the mess from last night."

"What makes you think Alecto will help us?" Jeno asked.

"My father always takes me…used to take me… to the Necromanteion once a year to talk to her," Lajos said. "She's always met with us. I'm sure she will again."

"The Necromanteion?" Gertie asked.

"It's the Oracle of the Dead, in Parga. A long way from here," Nikita said.

"It's another entrance to the Underworld," Jeno added. "But it's guarded by Cerberus."

"I was just telling Hector about how I was planning to go after the conflict is over, and he asked me if I could take you all today. He said we could fly and be back tonight to fight."

Jeno sighed. *I hope we can trust this demigod.*

Me, too, Gertie said.

In front of Hector's parked Mini Cooper, Gertie, with Apollo's lyre looped around her upper arm, hooked elbows with Jeno and Hector. On the other side of Jeno, Nikita hooked elbows with Jeno and Lajos. Gertie had been super shocked when Nikita hadn't insisted on flying on Gertie's back with her eyes closed and her arms tight around Gertie's neck. Apparently, Nikita cared about what Lajos thought of her.

I only care about saving my brother, Nikita told her. *Don't worry. Once we're flying, I'll return to our regularly scheduled programming.*

So long as you aren't strangling me and damaging my eardrums, I'm okay with that, Gertie said telepathically.

Jeno laughed out loud. The two demigods on either end both looked at him.

"What's so funny?" Hector asked.

Nikita's face turned bright red.

"Nothing, really," Jeno said.

Ah, Hector said to them, even though he wouldn't be able to hear their telepathic replies unless they specifically spoke to his mind. *I guess I won't be in on the private jokes anymore.*

I'll try to include you when I can, Jeno said.

"This is turning out to be a better day than expected," Lajos said, ignorant of their quiet exchanges. "I'm under the protection of the helm of invisibility and about to fly without a plane." In his mind, he added (not realizing three of them could hear it), *Your timing couldn't have been any better.* "It's nice to actually see you all, to have a face with the voice."

"Are we ready for lift off?" Jeno asked.

"Let's go!" Lajos said eagerly.

Jeno and Gertie leapt up into the sky, with Jeno leading the way. Nikita closed her eyes and screamed.

The heavy frames of Hector and Lajos drooped on either end of the band of flyers as they ascended into the air. Hector didn't like the feeling of dragging by Gertie's elbow, so he swung his free arm around her waist and traveled backward. He pulled his other arm from her elbow and encircled her waist, laying his cheek against her heart, which began to beat a bit more erratically.

God, she'd missed being in his arms.

She erected a block around her mind as soon as the thought had escaped her. Hector hadn't heard it, but Jeno had. And so had Nikita.

But Nikita was too busy screaming.

When they were a few hundred feet in the air, which was a comfortable place to Gertie because they were above the undercurrents but below the upper, they leveled off and moved forward. The sky had become overcast, which disappointed Gertie. She'd hoped to fly beneath a bright sun while under the protection of the helm. She missed its brightness even though her memories of its stinging touch made her shiver.

Nikita peeked at the ground below and shouted, "Why so high? Can't we go a little lower?"

She didn't understand about the currents and the birds.

"Oh, gods," Lajos said nervously. "I think I'm too heavy for Nikita. I think she's going to drop me!"

"Do what I did," Hector called out from his end of the line toward Lajos. "This is much more comfortable."

Lajos leaned back to see what Hector had done. Then he swung his outside arm around Nikita's hips and clung to her.

Nikita was shocked when Lajos's face pressed into her boobs (it was an accident, but still!). His uncensored thoughts in reaction to that shocked her even more. In this state of surprise, she accidentally slipped her arm from Jeno's elbow.

Immediately, she and Lajos began to fall from the sky.

Nikita and Lajos both screamed.

And then, of course, it started to rain.

Jeno raced down with the others toward the plummeting couple, all the while telling Nikita telepathically, *You can fly! You still have the vampire virus running through your veins. You just have to use your will to stop yourself from falling.*

But Nikita just continued to scream and to fall with Lajos clinging to her.

"It burns!" Nikita shouted.

Gertie was frantically trying to figure out how to take possession of her friend. If she could control her, maybe she could save her.

Suddenly Jeno let go of Gertie to catch the falling couple with both hands, and the sunlight stung her. Because of the fresh rain, Nikita and Lajos slipped from Jeno's grasp. He tried again. At last, he got hold of them. Both Nikita and Lajos clung to Jeno, nearly knocking the helm from his head.

Gertie raced toward him with Hector in her arms and grabbed hold of Jeno's leg. The relief from the sunlight was immediate.

"I'm so sorry! So sorry!" Nikita repeated over and over as she and Lajos gasped for air. "Thank you, Jeno! Thank you, thank you, thank you. You're my hero. Thank you, thank you, thank you."

"You're my hero, too, Jeno," Lajos said.

In spite of the scare and the pain she had just endured, Gertie laughed. When Hector saw that she was okay, he laughed, too.

"I've lived a long time and thought I'd done it all," Jeno said, still sandwiched between the two panting mortals. "Apparently not."

Gertie laughed some more—it felt good for a change—and held on to both Jeno and Hector as they soared northwest across Greece toward Parga in the cool, sprinkling rain.

After about two hours had passed, during which Gertie had kept a block around her thoughts (how could she not in Hector's arms, causing her all kinds of feels, especially when she could read his uncensored mind?), Jeno interrupted her thinking and said, "That's Patras below, where we first met."

The rains had cleared, and she was still holding onto his leg, and she now looked up at him and gave him a gentle smile. Who would have known the boy on the bus would have come to mean so much to her?

She let down her guard, so he could soak in that thought, and then she erected the wall around her again. She did it because Hector was thinking that he didn't care that she was a vampire. Holding her in his arms again reminded him how much he loved her, and he couldn't imagine ever feeling this way about another.

Gertie did not want her reaction to Hector's thoughts overheard by Jeno, but she couldn't prevent him from overhearing Hector's.

It can happen, Gertie heard Jeno say to Hector telepathically. *Feeling that way about another. But it can take a very long time.*

I'm sorry, Jeno, Hector replied. *I keep forgetting that you have access to my every thought.*

Is that a polite way of telling me to stay out of your head? Jeno asked.

Hector chuckled, which made Gertie laugh a little, too.

Nikita's screams had softened to a quiet whine, which she uttered softly into Jeno's neck. Lajos's face was near hers, but he was no longer afraid now that he was holding on to the more solid form of Jeno. In fact, Lajos had spent the majority of the flight contemplating the environment. From his thoughts, Gertie had gathered that he was concerned about endangered species and forests, and that seeing everything from this perspective added to his fear of the impact of human development on the rest of the environment. But his ruminations were soon replaced by a growing interest in studying Nikita. He thought she was cute and was enjoying his close view of her soft eyelashes and pretty pink lips. He liked observing Nikita as much, if not more, than the environment below.

"What are you thinking about?" Hector asked Gertie.

"I don't know, why?"

"You're smiling," he said. "It's nice to see."

Very softly, she whispered, "I think Nikita and Lajos like each other."

He glanced up at them. "He does seem into her."

"I can hear you," Nikita complained.

"Oops." Hector laughed.

Luckily, Lajos seemed ignorant of their conversation.

"We need a plan," Jeno said.

"Any ideas?" Hector asked.

"Maybe." Jeno turned a little more to the west, now that they had passed Patras. "The last time I visited the Necromanteion, about twenty or so years ago, there were tour guides taking people in and out of there."

"That's still true today," Lajos said. "My father and I always hired a boat and took the Acheron up where it meets the Cocytus. Then we banked at the cove and walked up to the monument. We always went at night, when the tourists were gone, but they'll be there today."

Hector glanced toward Helios, who still had a long way to go before setting in the west. "We can't afford to wait until dark."

"Agreed," Jeno said.

"Why can't we just hide beneath the helm?" Lajos asked.

Jeno frowned. "I think people will hear us."

"Maybe they'll think we're ghosts," Nikita said.

Hector nodded. "Not a bad idea."

"No, listen," Jeno said. "There's no reason for us all to use the helm. Gertie and I are the only two who need it."

"What about me?" Nikita asked.

"I can tell by the tint of your eyes and skin that the virus in your blood has nearly worn off," Jeno said. "The sun shouldn't hurt you anymore."

"So, you want the three of us to walk there on foot, along with the tourists?" Lajos asked.

"I think that would be best," Jeno replied.

"I'm all for walking." Nikita gave them a cheesy grin.

"This means we need to stop at the harbor in Parga and rent a boat," Hector pointed out.

"That makes sense," Gertie said. "The three of you would look pretty suspicious just showing up on the bank out of thin air."

So Hector rented a boat. Gertie and Jeno decided they would ride with them, rather than fly, because they were tired. They weren't nearly as bad off as the mortals, who were sleep deprived and starving. As they were all about to climb in at the dock, Jeno suggested that the others eat a quick meal.

"We don't know what we'll be up against," Jeno said, "and then there may not be another chance."

Gertie and Jeno waited in the boat beneath the helm while the mortals went to a food stand. She overheard Lajos complain about the Styrofoam and how bad it was for the environment. Although the boat was tied to a dock, the riverbank was nearby and covered in weeping willows with branches still wet from the recent rain. The look of the river reminded her of the TV show about swamp people and alligator hunters in the Louisiana swamp land.

Out of the blue, it seemed to Gertie, Jeno said, "I think you should be with Hector."

There were no others around them, so he spoke out loud, probably because he had blocked her out of his mind.

She studied him for a moment, trying to decide what to say to that, because she wasn't sure how it made her feel. What was the use of being with Hector when she would outlive him and then be lonely for the rest of her existence? Jeno had hinted that maybe they could reconnect after Hector passed, but that was just too strange for Gertie to consider. She believed in the idea of being with one person, one true love. Yes, if things were different, she would not hesitate to choose Hector. She was blocking these thoughts from Jeno and allowing herself to admit that if she could have Hector, she would take him. But she had to think practically, and since she also loved Jeno—not the same way she loved Hector, but still—she would be better off with someone who would live with her eternally.

And she already knew how Hector felt about being turned. He'd executed too many vampires for doing that very thing. It was against the laws created by the gods and enforced by the demigods, and he would feel like a hypocrite if he broke them.

Didn't Jeno remember how badly it had hurt him when the woman he had loved for thirty years had left this world? Jeno had once admitted that he had contemplated suicide after that, because he thought he would never find love like that again. And then he had met Gertie on the bus.

Was it possible she could endure that, too? If she chose Hector, could there still be life for her later, after he'd gone?

Gertie felt so overwhelmed that tears formed in her eyes and she sniffled.

At that moment, a thick vine twisted up from a grassy embankment near the dock and grew up toward their boat. Jeno and Gertie glanced at one another and then turned and stared at the vine. The leafy structure seemed to be staring through the helm right at her.

Gertie had come to associate vines with her father, Dionysus. Is that what this was all about? But she was beneath the helm. He couldn't see her, right? Involuntarily, she sniffled again.

She and Jeno were startled when the end of the vine reached out erratically and snatched the helm from Jeno's head. Then it recoiled and disappeared into the grassy embankment.

The two vampires immediately began to burn, writhing in pain. Jeno grabbed Gertie's arm and pulled her overboard into the river and away from the direct sunlight.

It took a few seconds to recover from the shock and the sting, and the moment she did, she wondered what had just happened. Had Dionysus just stolen the helm?

CHAPTER ELEVEN

The River Nymphs

Beneath the water, Jeno reached over and took Gertie's hand. *Are you okay?*

Yes. But what the heck just happened?

Dionysus.

So Jeno had suspected the same thing as Gertie. *What do we do now?*

They could see and speak telepathically to one another, but most of their other senses were blunted by the water. Gertie tried to reach out to sense Hector and the others. She got nothing. Then the bottom of the boat above them moved away from the dock and headed up the river.

They probably think we're still with them beneath the helm, Jeno speculated.

So I guess we should follow the boat and figure out what to do when we get there.

Side by side, Gertie and Jeno swam beneath the boat wondering how they would manage now without the helm. They hadn't gotten very far along when the weeds on the riverbed below seemed to be closing in on them.

Those aren't weeds, Jeno said.

Then what are they?

River nymphs.

Their long, flowing dark hair had resembled water weeds dancing in the current. Now that they were closer, Gertie recognized faces—a dozen beautiful faces—and other human characteristics. Like vampires, they wore no clothes, but they didn't create illusions to hide that fact.

Only their long, flowing hair covered most of the parts Gertie was glad not to see.

As the nymphs surrounded the two vampires, Gertie asked, *Should I be worried?*

I am, he replied, taking her hand.

A shimmering golden halo stretched out from the nymphs and encompassed Gertie and Jeno in the water. It felt warm and strange. Gertie bit her lip and tried not to show how frightened she was.

"Geia sas," the nymph said.

Gertie understood the Greek phrase for "hello," but she was shocked that she could hear the creature at all, because vampires were normally audio impaired underwater.

It's her spell, Jeno explained, still holding her hand. *The gold light is a conductor.*

"Is that Apollo's lyre?" the nymph said to her in Greek.

The nymphs would have to destroy her to steal the lyre. "What? This old thing?"

"Are you saying I'm mistaken?" the nymph challenged Gertie.

"No, I mean…" Gertie hesitated. "What if I *were* saying that?"

"Then you would be lying," the nymph said. "Because I know Apollo's lyre when I see it. None other has the golden tortoise shell as its base. I only asked the question as a way of opening a polite conversation."

"Oh, well, then. I'm sorry, but you can't have it. You'll have to kill me first."

"Apollo loaned it to us," Jeno explained. "For a very important reason."

"We don't wish to take it," the nymph said, smiling. "We wish to hear you play on it."

The knot in Gertie's belly relaxed.

"Neither of us play," Jeno said.

"Apollo would never loan his lyre to someone who can't play." The nymph moved closer. "Perhaps you stole it."

"No," Gertie insisted, the knot returning. "He gave it to us to give to our friend, Hector. He's the one who plays and sings."

"And where is Hector?" the nymph asked.

Gertie looked up at the boat that had already traveled several yards up the river without them.

In a whirlwind of confusion, the nymphs grabbed Gertie by the wrists and pulled her and Jeno through the river toward the boat. They didn't swim in a straight line, but rather swirled in loops with the currents beneath the river, like they were riding a roller coaster. Gertie spun and rolled out of control before coming to a sudden stop just as the nymphs flung themselves—all of them—toward the boat and tipped it over.

Hector, Lajos, and Nikita plunged into the water. They were startled but ready to fight for their lives.

Hector and Lajos pulled out their swords and pointed them toward the nymphs. Instead of fighting back, the nymphs broke out in boisterous laughter.

"Put away your weapons," the leader, who'd been doing all the talking, said. "We will offer you safe passage in exchange for a song."

Gertie turned to Hector. "They want to hear you sing and play on Apollo's lyre."

Nikita and the two demigods couldn't breathe and needed air. All three floundered to the surface, but the long tendrils of hair from the river nymphs held them back.

"They can't breathe!" Gertie cried out in alarm.

A silver halo emanated from the nymphs, and Nikita, Hector, and Lajos stopped struggling. The silver halo was like a magical bubble of air that allowed the humans to breathe underwater.

"Is that better?" the river nymph asked.

"It's amazing," Lajos said. "Absolutely incredible."

"Now for that song," the nymph prodded.

Gertie handed Apollo's lyre to Hector. She heard his thoughts as he sifted through the list of songs he knew, trying to choose one he thought would please the nymphs. Then he held the lyre and strummed it with his fingers. The sound the strings produced was incredibly beautiful, and it carried more clearly in the water than Gertie had expected.

Then Hector began to sing (to hear Hector's song, go here: https://soundcloud.com/travispohler/dreamer):

Before you close your eyes,
After you shut the door and you turn out the lights,
Remember all the days gone to waste.
Let 'em go, your shoulders know sleep's your only break.
And stay a dreamer, every day.
Dream every moment you're awake.
You may feel so far from space,
But someday the stars will remember your name.

Before you accept your fate,
After you got a job and your dreams are far too late,
Remember all the days gone to waste.
Don't hesitate, surely your job can wait, live for today.
And stay a dreamer, every day.
Dream every second you're awake.
Money will mean nothing in the grave.
You'll die no matter how much you're paid.

Dreamer,
The ground's so far beneath you.
Dreamer,
Someday they'll believe you.

The whole time Hector was singing, Gertie's heart had felt like it would explode. He was so freakin' incredible and sexy and sweet.

And he was in love with her. He could have anyone he wanted, and he wanted her.

If only she weren't a vampire.

As his song came to an end, she saw she wasn't the only one captivated by him. Fish of all kinds, turtles, ducks, and other living creatures of the river, had come closer to listen to the beautiful voice singing with Apollo's lyre. And the river nymphs had gathered so close to Hector, that Gertie could no longer see him. Their long tendrils of hair had wrapped around him and shielded him like the drooping leaves of a willow.

Her stomach knotted up again in fear.

What were they doing? Why were they so close to him?

Gertie tried to read their thoughts, and, although they were jumbled, she began to pick up on some. The nymphs were enamored. Maybe obsessed. They didn't intend to keep their promise of safe passage up the river.

They're going to take him, Jeno warned. *We've got to get him out of there.*

Oh no! Can you mesmerize them or something? She bit her lip.

Not under water.

In full-blown panic, she charged the cluster of nymphs and shouted, "You promised safe passage!"

"We didn't swear on the river," they began to chime. "We didn't swear on the river."

"Lajos, help!" Gertie cried.

Lajos and Nikita floundered through the water toward her and Jeno, and together they clawed through the nymphs, whose swirling movements and flowing hair made it difficult to fight them. The nymphs controlled the current of the water, and Gertie was forced to flip and roll as she struggled to get to Hector in the middle of them all.

"Hector!" Gertie screamed.

And suddenly she knew she could never live without him.

"Hector!" she cried again.

She was pulled by her ankles down to the bottom of the river away from Hector and the nymphs. She could no longer see Jeno or Nikita or Lajos—only the slimy bottom of the riverbed as her body scraped along its surface. She felt along the slimy bottom for something to grab onto, to stop herself from being pulled away. Her nails clawed, but nothing held. Then she opened her mouth and sank her fangs into the earth.

That stopped her, even though it had nearly ripped out her jaw to do it. Her feet came free and she pulled her fangs free, too. Then she searched in the darkness for the others. She could see, but she heard nothing, and she wasn't sure in what direction she should go.

Then out of the haze, something swam toward her. It was Jeno, her knight in shining armor. He grabbed her wrist and led her back to the swarm of nymphs.

Together, she and Jeno swam through the twisting bodies and swirling hair once more toward the center and toward Hector, only to be pushed and shoved away again.

Nikita came rolling through the river toward Gertie, with Lajos just behind. They were all four being repelled again and again by the barrier of nymphs surrounding their friend.

Then Hector's voice carried the song once again through the water, and the nymphs stilled. Their hair detangled and fell away from Hector, and Gertie saw him there, in the center, singing his heart out. As he sang and played the lyre, and while the nymphs were mesmerized, she and Jeno inched their way to the center beside him. Lajos and Nikita followed their lead.

Now what? Gertie said to Jeno once the five of them were treading side by side.

I don't know.

Great. They were trapped inside a circle of crazy nymphs who seemed bent on keeping Hector for themselves.

When the song ended, Hector quickly began another, to keep the nymphs from closing in. This time he sang a prayer to his father.

But before he had finished the first refrain, something wrapped itself around Gertie's ankles again and pulled. This time, her friends were pulled down with her—down, down, down into the depths of the river and along the slimy bottom. The river nymphs screamed in protest and chased after them but whatever had a hold of Gertie and her friends was too fast for the nymphs.

Gertie could sense Hector, Nikita, and Lajos struggling to hold their breath. Now that they were outside of the magic of the nymphs, they couldn't breathe. Gertie extended her fangs to try her trick of piercing them into the bottom of the river again, but as she stretched open her mouth, whatever had been pulling her came to a stop. Jeno was right beside her, and Nikita, Hector, and Lajos were scrambling for the surface to breathe. She and Jeno followed them.

When she surfaced, she braced herself for the burning pain of the sun, but there was none. They had entered a cave only partially illuminated by light seeping in through cracks.

She plunged her face back into the water and scoured the area for any sign of having been followed—by either the nymphs or whatever had rescued them (if, indeed, that's what had happened at all. For all she knew, this cave was just another trap). As she scanned the riverbed with her acute vampire vision, she had a shock that made her face flood with heat and made every inch of her skin tingle. A face looked up at her from the bottom of the river, and it looked exactly like the face of her grandmother.

CHAPTER TWELVE

The Necromanteion

Gertie dived down into the river toward the slimy bottom in search of what she thought was her grandmother. She scanned the river floor but found no sign of the lovely face that used to comfort her.

Jeno came up from behind her. *Why would your grandmother be in this river?*

I know what I saw.

Come with me. We've made it into the Necromanteion, not far from the gate where Cerberus stands guard.

She reluctantly followed him back to the surface and climbed out onto the rocky bank of the river in the quiet cave with the others. Saving Klaus had to be her priority right now.

"That was crazy," Nikita said, panting. "I didn't think we'd make it."

"I wonder what got us out of there," Lajos said.

"It had to be someone powerful," Jeno said.

Hector reached out and touched Gertie's arm. "Where's the helm, guys? Please don't tell me you lost it back there with the psycho nymphs."

"We didn't," Jeno said.

"Thank the gods." Hector took a deep breath.

"Dionysus took it," Gertie said. "At least, we think it was him."

"What?" Hector's mouth dropped open as she told him about the vine. "What are we going to tell Hades?"

"The truth," Jeno said.

Hector didn't say it, but he was thinking it would be harder to negotiate for Klaus's soul without the helm.

"I'm going to call to my mother," Lajos said.

As he closed his eyes and held up his palms, Gertie closed hers, too, and tried to talk to her grandmother.

Aphrodite said you weren't dead. Are you in the Underworld? I miss you so much. I even thought I saw you. Impossible, I know.

She opened her eyes a moment later when she sensed a presence. Only the five of them stood in the cave. But then twinkling lights appeared, blinking on and off, like fireflies.

"That's her," Lajos whispered. "I recognize her light. She's coming."

The blinking lights moved closer. Once they were less than twenty feet away, a woman—or creature—stepped toward them. Her golden eyes were fierce, and her red hair was spiked, longer and more dramatic than Nikita usually wore hers. On the tip of each of her pale green wings, as thin as paper, was a sharp, curved claw. A thick snake curled around her neck, its head pointed in their direction, as though about to strike.

"Mother," Lajos said. "Did you hear about my father?"

She moved closer to Lajos and put her arms around him while her snake nestled under his chin. "I'm sorry for you. He is here, in the Elysian Fields. He was a good man."

Tears came to the boy's eyes, but he wiped them away and faced his mother. "I've come to ask a favor."

"You've never asked me for anything, in your entire life," she said. "I hope I can give you what you need."

Lajos smiled. "These are my friends." He introduced each of them. "This is Alecto, the Unceasing."

Nikita was trembling like a leaf, and even Gertie felt afraid before the Fury. Alecto was kind to her son, but she looked terrifying.

"Ares killed Nikita's brother, Klaus," Lajos went on.

"He'd been possessed by a vampire," Gertie blurted out. "Klaus was innocent."

"I'd like a chance to sing in exchange for Klaus's soul," Hector added.

"Someone will have to take his place," Alecto said. "The Fates won't allow anything less."

"I'll do it," Gertie said, as her body went numb. It was pretty surreal to offer yourself up to a god. She tried not to think about it.

"No." Hector stepped forward. "I'll do it."

Gertie read Hector's mind. He thought since he couldn't be with her, since she was a vampire and it was against the law to turn him, he didn't have much to live for anyway.

And Gertie would rather die than be left behind by Hector.

"It should be me," Jeno said.

"Hades will decide," Alecto said. "Come."

The Fury turned and led them down the dark and winding tunnel from which she had emerged. Nikita reached out and held Gertie's hand.

Gertie squeezed it. "It's going to be okay."

"I don't want anyone else to have to die to save Klaus," she whispered. "Maybe it should be me."

"No," Gertie said loudly. "Your parents wouldn't be able to handle that. Please don't even think of it."

Nikita frowned.

"Promise me," Gertie demanded.

"Okay," Nikita whispered. "I promise. But I don't want to lose you, either. Promise me I won't lose you."

Gertie didn't reply.

She noticed Lajos take Nikita's other hand, and Nikita gave him the only smile she could muster under the circumstances.

As they reached a bend in the tunnel, Cerberus, the three-headed guard dog, came into view. He was massive, like his sister, the Hydra.

She wondered if he recognized her from the last time she had come to his gate, with Charon.

"You better start singing now," Alecto said to Hector.

Hector strummed the strings of Apollo's lyre, which immediately brought an air of calm to the cave. Soon, his voice carried, too (to hear Hector's song, go here: https://soundcloud.com/travispohler/dreamer):

Before you close your eyes,
After you shut the door and you turn out the lights,
Remember all the days gone to waste.
Let 'em go, your shoulders know sleep's your only break.
And stay a dreamer, every day.
Dream every moment you're awake.
You may feel so far from space,
But someday the stars will remember your name.

As he sang, bats emerged, one by one, from the darkness to listen. Then other creatures—rats, spiders, and snakes. Gertie shivered. Then Charon appeared on his raft, looking totally captivated.

Before you accept your fate,
After you got a job and your dreams are far too late,
Remember all the days gone to waste.
Don't hesitate, surely your job can wait, live for today.
And stay a dreamer, every day.
Dream every second you're awake.
Money will mean nothing in the grave.
You'll die no matter how much you're paid.

Dreamer,
The ground's so far beneath you.
Dreamer,
Someday they'll believe you.

Cerberus had fallen asleep, and the gate now opened, and two figures emerged. Gertie recognized Hades and Persephone. They hovered above the surface of the river.

"That was breathtaking," Persephone said. "Bravo, young man."

"You again," Hades said. "Do you have my helm?"

"It was stolen by Dionysus," Gertie replied. "We were on our way to bring it to you when he took it."

"We were just on the shore of Parga," Jeno added. "We promise to do whatever it takes to get it back."

"If you don't have my husband's helm, then why have you come?" Persephone asked.

"They want to make a trade," Alecto explained. "A soul for a soul."

Gertie started to tell Persephone and Hades what she knew about Orpheus, but Hades cut her off. "Don't mention his name in my kingdom ever again."

"I came to sing for you, Lord Hades," Hector said.

"I'd rather have my helm," the lord of the Underworld complained. "Bring it to me, and then we'll talk about a trade."

"But how?" Gertie asked. "How can we get it from Dionysus?"

"Try working with another of his enemies," he said just before he and Persephone vanished.

Nikita burst into tears.

"It's going to be okay," Gertie said, even though she didn't believe it herself. She put an arm around her friend.

"I don't understand," Hector murmured. "Hades said he would help us if we gave him Athena's shield—which we did."

"We also said we'd return the helm," Jeno pointed out. "I believe he will help us, once we do."

"But how can we get it now?" Hector asked.

"Go to Queen Hera," Alecto suggested.

At that moment, Cerberus awakened and growled at them, angry that they had come so close to his gate. He climbed to his feet. All three heads snapped at them.

The teens backed away, and as they hiked in the direction they had come, Lajos asked his mother, "So how do we find Queen Hera?"

"Look for Iris, her messenger," Alecto said.

"And where do we find *her*?" Gertie asked.

"In any rainbow," the Fury said. "Now I must get back to work."

Lajos took her hand. "When will I see you again?"

"Keep your father's tradition," she said. "Visit me here each year."

"Any chance you can take me to see him?" Lajos asked.

She stopped and put her arms around him, the snake eerily nestling his chin again. "I'm afraid not. Now be strong and go save your city."

The Fury kissed her son on the cheek and then flew away, vanishing into a myriad of twinkling little lights.

Lajos brushed tears from his eyes and said, "Let's go save Athens."

It must be hard to see your mother only a few minutes each year, Gertie thought. *But at least he knows she loves him.*

As the five teens walked along the tunnel of the Necromanteion, Gertie was plagued with worry. How would she be able to look for Iris in a rainbow when she couldn't tolerate sunlight?

Rainbows touch down into the sea from the clouds, Jeno said in response to her thoughts. *We'll swim out to sea in search of one.*

She looked up at him and smiled. That actually made sense. From what Gertie had read, Iris was the goddess who maintained the balance of nature by refilling the clouds with water from the sea.

She's also a goddess of harmony and Hera's messenger, Jeno added.

Nikita still held Gertie's hand and was sobbing uncontrollably. She'd lost faith in their ability to save her brother and was grieving.

Gertie had decided not to keep telling Nikita it would be okay. Because maybe it wouldn't be okay.

Hector came up between them. "So we still have a few hours before dusk, but I don't think I can just wait around in this cave."

"Me either," Gertie agreed.

"But how will we get back?" Lajos asked. "They can't be in the sun."

"We could swim," Hector said. "I'm really fast in the water, and so are these two." He flicked a thumb toward Gertie and Jeno. "With the three of us towing you two, we could make it back to Patras by nightfall and then fly the rest of the way."

Nikita shuddered. "What about the psycho nymphs?"

Gertie had been wondering the same thing.

"You three take a boat from Parga," Jeno said. "Gertie and I are going to go look for Iris. Then we'll meet you in Athens tonight."

"I don't think we should split up," Hector said.

"I like the idea," Nikita said. "As scared as I am of heights, I'm more frightened of drowning. Those nymphs nearly did us in."

"She's got a point," Lajos said.

Gertie met Hector's anxious look. She didn't want to leave him any more than he wanted to leave her. "Jeno's right. We should split up."

Hector's mouth became a thin line.

"I promise we'll be careful," Jeno said. "I'll keep her safe."

Hector clasped Jeno's arm. "Thanks, brother." Then he put an arm around Gertie, kissed her cheek, and said, "Be careful."

CHAPTER THIRTEEN

The Rainbow Goddess

The river nymphs were waiting for them when Gertie and Jeno dived into the water from the deep cave of the Necromanteion. When the nymphs realized neither Hector nor Apollo's lyre was with them, they rolled away with the current and disappeared into the surrounding weeds. Gertie hoped they wouldn't think to upset the boats leaving Parga.

As she and Jeno swam toward the sea, Gertie couldn't stop herself from searching for her grandmother's face. She knew she'd just been imaging things, but her eyes combed the riverbed anyway. She noticed many snakes, fish, and plant life, but nothing among them even remotely resembled the kind and loving face that had brought her comfort all her life.

Soon the ground dropped below them several hundred feet, and the colors surrounding them became more varied. The water, too, changed. It became colder and saltier.

The Ionian Sea, Jeno told her. *But let's head for home and look for a rainbow on the way. Come on.* By home, he meant Athens.

They dodged a school of fish only to find a pair of dolphins had joined them—one on either side of them. Gertie and Jeno beamed at one another. After everything that had happened, the joy of swimming with dolphins uplifted their spirits.

The dolphins increased their speed, and Gertie and Jeno struggled to keep up.

You think they want to race? she asked him.

Have you noticed they slow down when we do? I think they like our company.

Gertie kicked her legs and gave it all she had. The four of them zipped through the sea.

When the dolphins leapt into the air and down again, they seemed to expect her and Jeno to do the same.

That's how we can check for the rainbow, Jeno said. *If we're quick, it won't even hurt.*

He mimicked the dolphin and leapt up and then dived back into the water.

Did it hurt? she asked.

Not really. Not much.

See anything?

No. Not yet.

I want to try.

She thought back to the nights when she and Jeno used to pass time in the Aegean doing this very thing. Those were days they'd never get back.

Moments like these remind me how glad I am to be alive, Jeno said. *Being with you, swimming with dolphins, and looking for rainbows…how romantic is that?*

She laughed and got a mouthful of water.

He jumped up again. *It only stings a little.*

She leapt into the air and quickly searched the skies as she made an arc over the water and re-submerged. *You're right. It doesn't hurt much. Maybe because we're soaked.*

They swam further out, taking turns leaping out of the sea for a look. The dolphins stayed with them.

It had rained earlier on their way to Parga. Gertie wondered if they could chase down that storm and find a rainbow in its wake.

Good idea, Jeno said. *This way.*

She followed Jeno across the Mediterranean toward the Aegean Sea, and after over an hour had passed without any rainbow sightings,

Alexander Island came into view. Not far from it was the teeniest hint of a rainbow. It wasn't very bright, and Gertie and Jeno weren't sure if it was a rainbow at all. As they swam closer to it, they could make out a small, winged creature, the size of a lap dog, with a golden pitcher in one hand. She was bound by vines at her ankles and wrists, and her golden wings flapped like those of a jarred moth.

"Help!" she cried.

Jeno and Gertie said goodbye to their dolphin friends and jumped up to the edge of the rainbow, where they found stair steps. The rainbow reminded Gertie of a catwalk, except it was arched, like what she imagined it must be like in the Gateway Arch in St. Louis, except there were no real walls—just bright, translucent colors. She and Jeno took the steps up toward the winged creature, relieved that the sunshine did not sting inside the rainbow.

"Oh, thank Zeus you found me," the goddess said in a high-pitched voice.

The vines were wound tightly around her wrists and ankles. Gertie and Jeno pulled at them and, when that did no good, they used their fangs to cut her free.

"Who did this to you?" Jeno asked, though Gertie suspected he knew the answer. Who else used vines as a weapon?

"I never saw his face," the goddess replied.

"Are you Iris?" Gertie asked.

"Yes, indeed. And who are you?"

"My name is Gertie," she said. "And this is my friend, Jeno."

"Gertie? Is your full name Gertrude Morgan?" Iris asked with wide eyes.

Gertie blanched. "Yeah. How did you know?"

"Oh, dear," the goddess said. She sat on a step above them, put down her pitcher, and rubbed her sore wrists. "That was fast. I don't know if I'm ready for this."

"For what?" Jeno asked.

The goddess studied Gertie's face. "Do you know who you are?"

"At one time, I thought I did. Now I'm not so sure. Why? Do you?" Her heart began to beat more rapidly, and her throat tightened. Why did Iris know her by name?

"I shouldn't say," Iris said. "Oh, what if I ruin everything?"

"Please?" Gertie asked. "I need to know. I'll do anything…"

Be careful, Jeno warned.

The winged creature fidgeted nervously. "Well, oh dear. Okay, then. Centuries ago, before the Olympians were born, I served Gaia, our mother earth."

"But now you serve Hera, right?" Gertie asked.

"That's right. When the Olympians overthrew the Titans, Hera claimed me for her servant. I do her bidding—in addition to refilling the clouds. It keeps me quite busy, but I'm fast, so I keep up."

"What has that got to do with Gertie?" Jeno asked.

"Not long after I became Hera's servant, there was rumor of a prophecy that I would one day be reunited with my mistress, Gaia, by the child of earth and vine."

"Gaia and Dionysus?" Gertie asked.

"That's what we thought for centuries," Iris said. "Gaia took every opportunity to mate with Dionysus in order to produce a child who might fulfill this prophecy."

"Gaia is really serious about having you back," Gertie muttered.

"Yes," Iris said. "Because when I was taken from her, well, nature became imbalanced. Some species are near extinction. Plants are dying off, too. The earth keeps getting hotter and hotter."

"That's true," Jeno said. "I've witnessed it myself."

Gertie shrugged. "I still don't see…"

"Gaia was rarely successful at getting Dionysus's attention, because only Ariadne has ever had his heart," the goddess said.

"Why can't you just leave Hera?" Gertie asked.

"It would be considered an act of treason," Iris replied. "I would probably be imprisoned in Tartarus with the Titan rebels."

"Gertie isn't a child of Gaia and Dionysus," Jeno said. "That would make her a goddess, which she isn't, or I wouldn't have been able to make her a vampire."

"Correct," Iris said. "However..."

"I am a child of Dionysus, right?" Gertie asked, eager for some affirmation of what she'd been sure of all along.

"Right," Iris said. "And your mother was Philomena, a daughter of Gaia."

"Was?" Gertie asked.

"She was killed before you were born," the goddess explained.

"How is that possible?" Jeno asked.

"Gaia sent Philomena to be with Dionysus during one of his nighttime parties with the Maenads and satyrs, which is quite dangerous. One never knows what the Maenads will do. They're unpredictable."

Jeno's face turned pale. Gertie squeezed his hand. Every time he thought of his mother, he filled with sadness, and now that his father was also gone, his reaction was worse.

"As always, Hera sent me to destroy the seed before a child could be conceived," Iris continued. "Hera hates Dionysus, because he's a reminder of her husband's infidelity."

"But it's not my father's fault," Gertie said. "Hera should punish her husband, not Dionysus."

Iris laughed. "If only it were possible to punish..." she didn't say his name. She cleared her throat. "Oh, dear."

"That's just as bad as what Athena did to Medusa," Gertie added. "Why do the gods go after the victims? It's so unfair."

"It *is* unfair," Iris said. "And, as the goddess of harmony, it goes against my nature to serve Hera in that way. Yet I have no choice."

"So what happened?" Gertie asked. "Obviously, you didn't destroy the seed of Dionysus in my case, or I wouldn't be here."

"Obviously," Iris agreed. "As I was refilling my pitcher that night, Gaia whispered to me that this child might be the one. So when Hera gave me her usual order, I secretly disobeyed."

Gertie swallowed hard. Her throat was so tight she could barely breathe.

"After Dionysus left Philomena, I went to her and took the newly formed baby from her womb and swallowed it. Then I transformed myself into a man, and I seduced a young woman who was walking alone at night in the ruins of the theater of Dionysus. Her name was Diane."

"My mother?" Gertie asked.

Iris nodded. "Afterwards, I told her she was carrying a child that didn't belong to her. I promised I would find her one of the wealthiest and most attractive husbands in the world, and that I would give her a happy life full of good fortune, if only she would bear this child and then return her to Athens before her eighteenth birthday."

Gertie's mouth fell open and her eyebrows lifted.

"I told her that the child's grandmother was a powerful goddess, and she would watch over the child and protect her entire family."

"My grandmother is..." Gertie couldn't say it. It seemed too impossible. She was sure she was either dreaming or hallucinating. She blinked several times, recalling her grandmother's face in the riverbed.

"Gaia," Jeno finished for her.

"Yes," Iris said.

Tears filled Gertie's eyes. "My grandmother is Mother Earth."

"Indeed," Iris said.

She tried to let that sink in.

"How did Philomena die?" Gertie asked.

"The Maenads," Iris said sadly.

"Oh." Gertie couldn't think. She was trying to process all this new information, but her head was spinning. "Why didn't my grandmother tell me? Why did I have to find this out from you? If I hadn't been looking for you, then..." She burst into tears.

Jeno put an arm around her.

"The Fates have shown us time and time again that we aren't to interfere," Iris said. "And yet we had. I think Gaia didn't tell you because she had already taken a chance by saving your life. She was afraid to tempt the Fates further."

"It would have been easier if I'd known the truth," Gertie insisted.

"Do you really believe that?" Iris asked.

Gertie thought about her parents and how disconnected she'd always felt from them, and yet there was this constant yearning to be loved and accepted by them—especially by her mother. If Gertie had known, maybe she wouldn't have always felt so broken-hearted over the two people who had raised her without love. And now, to find out the only person who had ever loved her had been lying to her all along—Gertie was overwhelmed.

"Why did my grandmother pretend to die?" Gertie asked suddenly.

"You need to ask Diane that question," Iris said. "That was her doing."

Gertie sucked in air. None of this made any sense. "And how am I supposed to reunite you with Gaia? I don't know the first thing about that."

"The prophecy didn't say," Iris said.

"So you don't know, either?" Jeno asked.

The goddess shook her head. "And we can't even be certain Gertie is the one."

"Iris, we came looking for you for a reason," Jeno said while Gertie processed all she'd been told. "Lord Hades loaned us his helm, and then it was taken from us by Dionysus. We were hoping you could send a message to Hera to help us find him and get it back."

"I'm afraid that's much too risky," Iris said. "The first thing Hera will want to know is who you two are and why you want the helm. If she figures out that Gertie is a daughter of Dionysus, she'll do everything in her power to stop you from whatever it is you're trying to do. She might even kill you both on the spot."

Gertie wanted to cry again, but she held back her tears. "We'll have to find him on our own, I guess. Can you give us any advice?"

"Now that I know he has the helm," Iris said, "I'm almost certain he was the one who bound me. And he probably did it so he could travel up my rainbow bridge to Mount Olympus and sneak through the gate undetected. I wouldn't recommend that you follow him, though."

Jeno had an idea. Gertie read his mind before he said it out loud. "Your rainbow bridge goes all the way to the Underworld, doesn't it?"

"Yes, why?" Iris asked.

"Can you show us the way?" he asked. "We need to tell Hades to go to Mount Olympus to reclaim his helm."

CHAPTER FOURTEEN

Mount Olympus

Gertie and Jeno waited a few steps from the bottom of the rainbow as Iris entered the realm of the dead to deliver their message to Hades. She hadn't been gone but a few seconds when suddenly the lord himself appeared on the rainbow bridge.

"Follow me," he said as he brushed past them.

Without saying a word, Gertie and Jeno climbed the steps after him.

He doesn't seem very pleased, Jeno noted.

I hope we aren't sending him on a wild goose chase.

On a what? Jeno's brows furled, and he paused for a moment before continuing up the steps.

Oh, sorry. That's an English expression. Never mind.

He read her mind and got the gist of it.

I have a really bad feeling, Gertie said.

I do, too. Something doesn't feel right about this.

Do you think Dionysus has created a trap? Gertie asked. *Maybe he's going to ambush us before we make it to Mount Olympus.*

Should we tell Hades? Jeno wondered.

I don't know. He's already so angry.

He'll be more so if we send him into a trap.

"Um, excuse me," Gertie said. "Lord Hades? What if Dionysus is planning…"

"Bring it," Hades said without missing a step.

Well, okay then, Gertie thought.

As they continued to climb toward Mount Olympus, she and Jeno looked down at the earth below. Dusk was beginning to settle. They had to hurry as fast as they could to help Hector and Lajos defend Athens against the next attack.

But Gertie was hoping to save Klaus first, if they could get back the helm.

When they reached the gates of Mount Olympus, Hades said, "Spring, Summer, Winter, and Fall, open the gates so that I, the lord of the Underworld, may enter with my prisoners."

Gertie and Jeno glanced at one another in shock. *Prisoners?*

A loud roar carried through the air, and a tunnel of cold wind lifted in front of them. At its center was a single rain cloud. As the wind settled and the rain cloud emptied its contents and then dissipated, the giant wall of clouds opened, and Hades moved forward.

"This way," he commanded.

They stepped from the rainbow and through the open clouds. The wall of clouds closed behind them, and, in front of them, at the center of a golden-paved plaza, was a round fountain spraying water into the blue sky from the spout of a statue of a golden whale. At the top of this fountain, where the water arched and fell into a pool bordered with golden bricks, was another rainbow. Gertie was in awe.

Behind this fountain was a giant palace of white stone and ornate columns. To the right and left of the palace were separate buildings, as tall, but not as wide or deep. One of the buildings had its golden doors latched open, revealing two golden chariots parked inside. The main palace of white stone was gilded and surrounded by a halo of gold. Rainbow steps led up to it.

"In here," Hades said as he climbed the rainbow steps up to the white stone palace.

Inside the massive hall was a circle of thrones, most of which were occupied by shining deities. They talked among one another. Two were arguing, but others were laughing. Three were singing softly at the feet of another. As soon as Hades entered the center of the room, the other gods noticed him, and all were silent. Gertie recognized Ares, Hermes, and Apollo, who sat to the right of the higher double throne, which must belong to Zeus and Hera, because the gods sitting on it were wearing crowns. An empty throne to the right of Apollo probably belonged to Poseidon (because of all the sea symbols), and to the right of it with a golden hammer in his hand had to be Hector's father, Hephaestus, though she'd only seen him in his animal form before now.

Gertie also recognized Aphrodite as the goddess who had others singing at her feet. They weren't singing now. Everyone's eyes were on the lord of the Underworld.

Hades held out his hand and said, "Come back to me."

The helm appeared and flew at lightning speed across the room and into Hades's outstretched hand. Standing newly exposed behind the double throne of Zeus and Hera was Gertie's father, Dionysus.

A collective gasp filled the room as the gods recognized a spy had been among them.

Hera stood from her throne and pointed an accusatory finger. "You!"

Zeus also stood. "Why have you done this?"

Dionysus moved to the center to face first Hades and then the others. "Well, it seems my invitations to Mount Olympus always get lost in the mail."

"How dare you come and spy on us!" Hera said in a shrill voice. "You know you're not welcome here."

"That's not fair," Gertie said without meaning to.

Everyone turned and looked at her.

Jeno said, *What the hell are you doing? Just apologize and fall down on your knees before you get yourself killed.*

No.

She met her father's eyes. His brow was arched in surprise. As Hera was about to reprimand her, Gertie stepped forward and asked, "Why do you gods always punish the victims?"

"How dare you?" Hera said in that shrill voice of reproach.

"Who is this girl?" another goddess, probably Artemis, asked.

"I'm sorry, but how dare *you*? You can't treat others this way," Gertie said to Hera, though not very loudly. Her throat seemed to close up, and she could barely get the words out. *I'm trading my soul for Klaus anyway,* she thought. *I'm basically dead already, so what's the harm in speaking the truth?*

Please don't, Jeno begged.

"Who are these prisoners you've brought forth...these vampires?" Zeus addressed Hades.

"Vampires? Here?" Athena asked.

"My name is Gertrude Morgan," Gertie said. "I'm a daughter of Dionysus and a granddaughter to Gaia."

Great, Jeno said. *Just ignore Iris's warning.*

"What?" Hera screeched.

"And a vampire!" someone pointed out. "They're both vampires, here on Mount Olympus!"

"Yes," Gertie said. "We're vampires. Not monsters. Not demons. But sensitive, intelligent, loving beings."

"I can attest to that," Aphrodite said from across the room.

"And, Queen Hera, you've been wronged," Gertie said in a thoughtful tone. "I'm sorry for how you've been mistreated. You've done nothing to deserve it." Her heart was beating out of control. Maybe she'd have a heart attack and die right there on the spot.

Hera now looked confused, as did Dionysus, who must have been wondering whose side Gertie was on. She wasn't sure how she felt about her father, but she had to speak her mind.

"Dionysus isn't the one who wronged you, though," Gertie said, unable to believe she'd been allowed to continue. She expected a lightning bolt to strike her at any moment.

"What is the meaning of this, Hades?" Zeus demanded. "I command you to explain yourself!"

Hades tucked his helm into the crook of one arm. "These two vampires are in collusion with Dionysus in the uprising in Athens."

"That's not exactly true," Apollo said from his throne.

Hades frowned. "They've admitted as much to me themselves."

Zeus pointed a long finger at Jeno. "You, there, lurking behind Hades. You tell us what this is all about."

Jeno cleared his throat and looked around the room. Gertie worried he was going to faint, but he surprised her by lifting his chin and speaking more loudly than she'd been able to so far. "Do you want the truth, Lord Zeus?"

"I expect nothing less," the god replied.

"You betrayed your wife, and Lord Dionysus was the result," Jeno said.

"Now wait a minute," Zeus interrupted.

"Let him speak," Hera insisted.

"Then, instead of taking up the matter with you, Queen Hera banished your son and my lord, Dionysus."

"He was a constant reminder," Hera interjected. "No one should have to live like that."

"You asked me to speak the truth," Jeno said. "So, because he was banished, Dionysus wanted to make himself some companions. He used his special wine to create the Maenads. My mother is one of them."

"Which one?" Dionysus asked.

Jeno turned another shade whiter and choked out, "Larissa."

Gertie could see Jeno faltering beneath the memories of his mother, so she said, "And the Maenads went home and destroyed their husbands and children. Remember? Jeno was one of them."

And Calandra, came Jeno's thought.

"And so Zeus ordered Dionysus to fix it," Gertie continued.

"I should have had those souls," Hades said. "They belonged to me. We wouldn't be in this mess had they been left to me."

"But we *are* in this mess," Dionysus said.

"We've been oppressed for centuries," Jeno said, regaining momentum. "With no economic resources and little help from the gods. We're the scourge of the human race, but we exist, and, except for those who've become bitter from our ill treatment, we aren't villains. We deserve the same freedoms as anyone."

"And I have a solution," Hades said. "Give the vampires to me. Make me their lord, as it should have been in the beginning."

Another collective gasp filled the room.

"What right have you to my people?" Dionysus challenged.

"Do you intend to destroy them?" Hermes asked. "Is that how you'll become their lord?"

"No." Hades shifted his weight to his other leg and lifted up his free hand as he spoke. "I want them to come and work for me."

"Enslavement?" Dionysus said. "That's your solution?"

"Not enslavement," Hades said. "Purpose. It's what they lack."

"Explain yourself," Zeus commanded.

"We all have a job to do, right?" Hades said. "No one is more a slave to his work than I, or my sons. Thanatos works night and day collecting souls, thousands of them."

He wants to make us soul collectors, Gertie thought.

Hades went on to explain his purpose for the vampires—how they could feed on the freshly dead bodies and get their sustenance without harming anyone, before escorting the souls to Charon. This would allow Thanatos, and even Charon and some of the others in his realm, a moment's rest.

"And I would give the vampires time to rest and enjoy themselves, too," Hades said. "They would be rich with the precious stones of my realm. They would become useful and respected and much better off in my kingdom."

"What do you vampires think of this proposition?" Zeus asked Gertie and Jeno.

They looked at each other. Gertie had mixed feelings.

"It sounds like a good solution," Jeno said. "But I don't know what the others will think."

"They might want a choice," Gertie said.

"A choice?" Hades echoed. "What choice did any of us have? I drew my lot and live with that consequence. I drew the Underworld. I had no choice in the matter."

"You could have chosen not to rule," a goddess, who'd been quiet up to that moment, pointed out. "My sisters and I were not offered the chance to draw lots. Over what realm do we rule? None."

Who's that? Gertie asked Jeno.

Hestia.

"That's a discussion for another time," Hades said. "Tonight, we must deal with the vampire dilemma. Athens is under attack. The vampires intend to turn as many mortals as they can to increase their army and their power. To prevent that from happening, I've unleashed my secret weapon."

What? Gertie turned to Jeno. *What secret weapon?*

"And what weapon is that?" Zeus asked.

"Medusa."

"So you're the one who stole my shield!" Athena accused.

"Someone had to do it," Hades said. "You had no right to Medusa's head."

The gods all started speaking at the same time. The palace floor shook from their anger.

Let's get out of here, Jeno said, turning himself invisible. The gods could still see him, but he was less conspicuous, and they were distracted.

Not knowing what else to do, Gertie followed his lead. She pulled in all her energy and stripped off her clothes. Then, tossing them aside, she and Jeno snuck out, in search of the rainbow bridge.

Your locket, Jeno said. *Cover it with your hand.*

She did as he said.

Coming toward the palace walls were three one-eyed giants.

Cyclopes, Jeno said telepathically. *Just stay close to me.*

Are the gods at war back there?

The entire mountain shook.

Sounds like it, Jeno said.

Gertie and Jeno approached the gate. The clouds wouldn't part to let them through. They could see Iris's rainbow on the other side, but they had no access out.

Now what? Gertie asked, trying not to panic.

I don't know. Jeno felt around the gate for a weak spot.

The palace walls shook, and sparks flew. Angry voices sounded throughout the mountaintop. Gertie and Jeno continued to feel all along the wall, searching for the place where the two sides of the gate came together, hoping they could use their powers to squeeze through.

They're going to notice we're missing, Jeno said. *Maybe we should go back, before we're caught.*

The ground shook violently, and the entire mountaintop lit up with the glow of a lightning bolt.

Holy crap! Gertie thought, biting her lips and frantically pushing on the impenetrable gate.

Just then, the clouds parted, and an enormous chariot entered. Standing at the reins was a large golden man with long, sun-bleached hair and an equally sun-bleached beard. He had massive shoulders and turquoise eyes.

That's Poseidon, Jeno said. *Let's get out of here.*

Poseidon stared down at them but did not stop them.

They slipped out and leapt into the evening sky for Athens.

To their horror, the entire city was in flames.

CHAPTER FIFTEEN

Stone Cold Terror

Athens was in flames.

Gertie and Jeno flew toward the acropolis, where the smoke was the thickest, and were shocked by what they found.

All the ancient ruins had been completely leveled, and worse, there were people, dozens of them, turned to stone. They'd been caught running, or cowering, or raising their hands defensively. One thing they all had in common was an expression of terror on their faces. Gertie and Jeno landed near where the Parthenon had once stood and looked around in stunned silence.

These people were newly turned vampires, Jeno said. *You can see their fangs. And I know that ravenous look anywhere. They were turned, and before they could have a proper feeding, they laid eyes on Medusa.*

I can't believe this. I just can't believe this.

Let's go look for Hector. But be careful.

Gertie tried to guard her thoughts, because all she could think of was Hector, and if he'd been turned to stone, she would lose it. If he'd been turned to stone, she'd do whatever it took to bring down the gods of Mount Olympus.

They leapt up from the rock and through the smoke and flew just above the city, scanning the landscape for signs of life, particularly signs of Hector, Nikita, and Lajos. Gertie's stomach was already as hard as a rock with the growing fear that she would have to return to New York City to tell Mamá and Babá that Klaus and Nikita were dead.

Please let Nikita and Hector and Lajos be okay, she prayed—to whom, she didn't know.

Everywhere they searched, they saw the stone statues of Medusa's victims. Not all had been turned to vampires first. Some had been humans running for their lives, or demigods with raised swords. Firefighters, policemen, and emergency medics stood frozen near their stalled vehicles, lights still flashing, without any sign of life. In the center of Omonoia Square were the poor beggars of the city, still human, but still as statues.

Had the entire city been turned to stone?

Gertie could no longer hold back her tears as she dreaded finding Hector and Nikita in the same condition as the others.

Jeno put an arm around her. "Don't give up hope."

They flew down closer to the streets when they neared the area where the Angelis apartment building had once stood. Here they saw more of the same. Black smoke lifted from most of the skeletal remains of buildings, but the flames had been reduced to embers. There was little left to burn.

"Let's try Hector's neighborhood," Gertie said. "Maybe he made it home."

They turned west toward the outskirts of the city, toward the suburbs. Vehicles were stalled all along the road. Gertie thought she saw movement in front of one of the houses in Hector's neighborhood.

"There." She pointed.

She and Jeno moved in closer and found an old man hobbling along the yard with a cane. He was in a state of panic. They landed beside him, and it was then that they noticed he was blind and fumbling around.

"Do you need help?" Jeno asked.

"Huh?" the man lifted his cane and swung it in the air defensively. "Who's there?"

"We're here to help," Gertie said. "We can take you to shelter, okay?"

"What's happening?" the man insisted. "Tell me what you see."

"The city's in flames," Jeno said. "The people are at war."

"Where are the others?" he asked. "They aren't all dead, are they?"

Gertie looked to Jeno, unsure of what to say, but he shook his head.

"Not all," Gertie said. "Please, let us take you inside."

The old man allowed them each to take an arm as they followed the sidewalk up to the door of a large house. Gertie rang the bell, and when no one answered, she opened the door and stepped inside.

"Hello?" Gertie called out, even though she sensed no one was present.

When they rounded the corner of the foyer, they had a scare: a woman with a look of shock on her stone-cold face stood as a warning. Her hands were about to cover her mouth, but she must have seen Medusa first.

The monster had made it into the suburbs. Gertie felt like throwing up.

They hid the old man down in the basement and found him a glass of water. He wanted to listen to the news on the television, but the electricity was out. Gertie and Jeno couldn't find him a radio, either.

"I'm sorry, but we have to go," Jeno said.

Gertie and Jeno scrambled into clothes they found in an upstairs bedroom before heading out.

They left the house for Hector's. Rather than fly, they ran through the streets, combing every yard and shrub for signs of their friends.

When they turned a corner, Gertie sensed another presence in the lawn. Something was moving in the shrubs near the front porch of the house in front of them. Gertie's pulse quickened as she imagined Medusa hiding, ready to spring at them. Should she close her eyes?

I don't think it's the monster, Jeno said. *Come on.*

Gertie followed Jeno as they neared the house. Gertie hoped beyond hope to find Nikita and Hector, but as they neared the shrubs, they found a mother and three small children.

"Please don't hurt us!" the mother begged. "Or take me, if you must, and spare my children!"

The four mortals—a mother, two elementary-school-aged sons, and a toddler daughter—were covered in ash and blood. They looked like they'd been through hell.

The scent of their blood reminded Gertie that she was hungry.

"We aren't here to hurt you," Jeno said. "Let's get you someplace safe."

Let's take them to the blind man, Jeno said telepathically. *They can hide in the basement together.*

A check of the mother's mind revealed her lack of trust, but who could blame her? Vampires had been wreaking havoc on the city all night. Why should she believe Jeno?

"We'll help you hide," Gertie said. "We really do want to help."

The mother picked up her little girl and held her on her hip, protectively. Without waiting for permission, Gertie picked up each of the small boys as Jeno took the mom and girl, and they ran with them in their arms two houses down to the blind man. They helped them all down into the basement, reassuring the blind man that his new guests were fellow survivors, and gave them pillows and blankets they found in other rooms of the house. In a gentle voice, Gertie told them to be very quiet and try to sleep.

"Don't come out until morning," Jeno said. "You'll be safe then."

The mother thanked them, trying not to shrink away in fear of them. Then Gertie and Jeno took off again.

About a block away from Hector's house, they sensed someone approaching from the air.

"It's about time you showed your face." It was Strophius, one of the older vampires from Crete. Although he wasn't as many centuries old as Jeno, he'd been turned in the days before the laws had been put in place by the gods. His physical appearance resembled a twenty-year-old. He landed in the street a few yards away.

"Strophius," Jeno said. "Where's the rest of your clan?"

"It seems the gods are set against us," the vampire replied.

"Who's in charge now?" Jeno asked.

"No one," Strophius said. "It's pure chaos. Vampires were turning people right and left, though as I'm sure you've seen, they've all been destroyed by Medusa."

"You aren't the only one left of your clan, are you?" Jeno asked.

"Unfortunately, I am. You're the first I've seen lately not made of granite."

"We're looking for our friends," Gertie said. "You're welcome to come with us."

"I'm just on my way back to Crete. I have friends there who didn't join the cause. Hopefully, they'll take me in."

"Be safe," Jeno said as Strophius flew away.

"Gertie? Is that you?"

Gertie turned to see Nikita running toward her in the next yard. Lajos was at her heels. The relief that went through Gertie brought tears to her eyes. She smiled and waved at Nikita. But where was Hector?

"Nikita, wait!" Hector called from inside the neighboring house.

Something's wrong, Jeno said telepathically. *Hector's mind is full of warning.*

Gertie studied the front porch of the neighboring house to see Hector emerge with Apollo's lyre. He was looking into the reflection of the round golden tortoise shell that formed the base of the instrument.

"I told you to stay with me!" Hector shouted.

"But it's Gertie!" Nikita hollered back with a smile on her face. "She and Jeno made it!"

Gertie ran toward her friend. Then she became aware of a presence on her trail—someone other than Jeno.

"Close your eyes!" Hector cried.

Jeno whipped through the air from behind Gertie toward Nikita.

To Gertie's horror, Nikita and Lajos stopped in their tracks, and their flesh shimmered with a loud cracking sound. Then their entire bodies became solid white stone. Their mouths and eyes were open, and their expressions showed their shock and surprise.

As Jeno landed in front of them—too late to block Medusa's stare—Gertie screamed, and Jeno, forgetting everything but the girl he loved, looked up and caught the gaze of the monster.

Gertie screamed again as Jeno turned to stone.

"Jeno!" Gertie shrieked.

The look on his face broke her heart.

"Turn around and look into my eyes," Medusa said in a throaty voice.

Gertie didn't turn around. She stood stiffly crouched, arms outstretched, ready to lift into the air if needed. She couldn't breathe.

"Run!" Hector cried.

Gertie took off across the yard toward Hector, with the monster on her heels.

Hector caught up to Gertie, wrapped an arm around her, and guided her away from the fierce monster at her back.

"This way!" he said.

Gertie could hear the monster following them as Hector led her to the back fence of the house he had just emerged from. They went through the gate and stumbled into a backyard swimming pool. They swam to the shallow end, and then Hector held up the lyre, turning in all directions, to see if Medusa had followed them into the yard.

"She doesn't like water," he said. "It took me a while to figure that out. She's been after me all night."

"That was Nikita!" Gertie cried, feeling numb and nauseous and about to faint. "That was Jeno!"

"There she is," Hector said. "Just stay in the water and don't look at her. She won't come after us in here."

"Hector, what are we going to do? What are we going to tell Mamá and Babá?"

"Look into my eyes!" Medusa called from the gate. "You can't resist me!"

"Listen to me, Gertie." Hector cupped her face with one hand. Water dripped from his wet hair and face, and she noticed a cut across his cheek that was bleeding. She fought the urge to lick it. "We have to concentrate on staying alive right now, okay?"

She burst into tears but wiped them away with wet hands as she nodded and said, "Okay."

Gertie looked at the reflection of Medusa in the golden lyre. Her gray skin resembled stone. The eyes in her sockets were solid white. The snakes that made up her hair hissed and curled around her head in a frenzied dance.

"The monster will move on," Hector said. "She's been chasing me all night, but if I stay long enough in one of these pools, she moves on. She always comes back for me, but, now that you're here, I've got a plan."

He pressed her close against him. She could feel his heart pounding, his lungs panting. He held Apollo's lyre in his other hand above their heads and kept turning in a circle, checking every direction for the monster, until he could no longer see her.

"I think she's left for more victims," he said.

"Hector, that was Jeno," Gertie repeated. "And Nikita and Lajos. What do we do? I can't believe it. I just can't believe it. Oh, my gods. What am I going to tell Mamá and Babá?"

Gertie couldn't stop trembling. Her teeth were chattering. She wasn't cold. She was terrified.

"This is what we're going to do," he said.

She stared off blankly—chattering, trembling, and numb.

"Gertie, look at me."

She met his eyes.

"First things first," he said. "I need you to bite me."

"What?"

"So I can fly. Please. Right now. Do it."

He put his hands on her waist and lifted his chin. She circled her trembling arms around his neck, stretched open her chattering teeth, and then pierced her fangs into his throat.

As numb and shocked and destroyed as she felt, the warm blood invigorated her. She closed her eyes and drank more than she should have—not quite a pint—which made her able to focus and to think clearly.

She wiped her mouth and had a realization. Jeno had been turned to stone, but he must still be alive; otherwise, why was she still a vampire? She looked up at Hector, who was just recovering from the paralyzing effects of her bite, and smiled.

CHAPTER SIXTEEN

In Hiding

W hat?" Hector asked her.

"I'm still a vampire. You know what that means?"

He thought for a second, and then he grinned. "Jeno can't be dead."

"That's right." Her smile widened. "Maybe none of them are. Maybe they're in some kind of temporary state."

"But if the sun hits them, will it…"

She frowned. "I hadn't thought of that." A lump rose to her throat. "I don't know."

"We can't save all the vampires, but we can try to save Jeno."

"How?"

"Come on."

He took her hand and leapt from the swimming pool into the cool night. In the air, he turned her around, so that they were flying flat on their backs.

"This is different," she said.

"This way, you can't look at anything directly," he explained. "It only takes a second for her to lock eyes with you."

"What if she jumps in the air and flies above us?"

"She hasn't been flying," he said. "She seems to be tied to the land. I don't know why. That's why I wanted you to bite me."

"So she avoids the sky and water," Gertie said. "Maybe she's avoiding Zeus and Poseidon."

Hector kissed the side of her face. "You're so smart."

Gertie studied Hector for a moment, drinking him in—figuratively this time. She hadn't allowed herself to remember how very attracted she was to him, but, just now, she couldn't help herself.

Hector chuckled.

She'd forgotten that he could read her mind. So much for him thinking it was wrong and invasive.

Touché, he thought.

He held Apollo's lyre above their faces and pointed it so that the golden base reflected the landscape below them. They maneuvered from the backyard to the front lawn and found their friends right where they had left them.

Hector's thoughts revealed that he wanted to move all three of them to his basement, where they would be well-hidden and safe from the sun. But the problem was flying with all three of them and using the lyre.

"Are you sure your basement's safe?" she asked him.

"I hope so. Can you think of a safer place?"

There was no way they could carry all three of them to New York. Plus, the sun would be rising soon, and if they got caught in it...she shuddered. Even taking them to a neighboring area, like Patras, would be risky. What if a stranger found them? She shook her head. "I guess not."

"We'll have to take them one at a time," Hector said. "You hold the lyre and navigate, while I carry them. I'll start with Nikita."

As they flew across the neighborhood toward Hector's house, Gertie wished with all her heart that Nikita was normal again, even if it meant listening to her screams and being strangled by her. Gertie did her best to use the reflection in the lyre to guide them safely, but it was awkward, and she wished she and Hector could switch jobs.

"You hold the lyre," she said. "I'm not used to this, and you've been doing it all night."

"True."

Hector took Apollo's lyre with one hand and handed over the bulky statue of Nikita, but as Gertie attempted to wrap her arms around her friend, lightning penetrated the sky, and a deluge of rainfall made the statue suddenly very slippery. Nikita slipped through Gertie's arms.

"Don't let her hit the ground!" Gertie screamed, as she and Hector zipped down and caught Nikita in the nick of time.

"Holy crap, that was close!" Gertie said as she sucked in air. She held her friend tightly against her chest.

The rain poured down hard on them, and they had to each hold one end of their friend as they, slowly and carefully, flew to Hector's house. Were the gods punishing them?

They entered through an upstairs window and sat Nikita down for a moment.

"I'm so tired of being soaked," Gertie said. She hadn't even dried from her swim across the ocean before Hector had made her jump into a swimming pool. Now she was dripping with rain as well.

"I'll get us some towels," he said, "even though we're going right back out in it."

"Get one for her, too."

Hector went to his bathroom next door, and, while he was gone, Gertie noticed the drawings he'd done of her last summer. They were still lying on his desk, along with a few more recent ones. Seeing them brought a sting to her chest, especially the one of the two of them being carried by Hephaestus as a giant white crane. That had been the most magical night of her life, and it seemed like so long ago.

Hector returned with the towels and brought her from her reverie. He must have been listening to her thoughts, because, without hesitating, and without saying anything, he gently wiped her face with the towel and then pressed his lips to hers.

She closed her eyes and kissed him back. All the longing washed over her as her lips pressed harder and harder against his. She kept thinking she should stop, but just couldn't. She needed him so badly.

After a few brief heavenly moments, he pulled away, and gave her the towel. "We better get moving."

It took her several seconds to recover, and then she wiped down Nikita before the two of them hefted her in their arms and hauled her downstairs. Although everything looked exactly as they had left it, the house felt haunted—not because Gertie sensed a presence, but because it was storming, and the memories of Hector's mother were fresh and biting. She tried not to read Hector's thoughts as they flew past his mother's bedroom downstairs toward the basement. It only made Gertie think of her own mother and all that Iris had revealed to Gertie that night. She hadn't had a chance to tell Hector.

He arched a brow at her, but she only said, "It's a long story. I'll tell you later."

They put Nikita in the corner of the room. Unlike the rest of the house, the basement wasn't fancy. It had a few comfortable pieces of furniture around a television, but it was mostly a storage area. Gertie took a blanket from a nearby recliner and wrapped it around Nikita, so she was better hidden, just in case. Then she and Hector made their way back to Jeno and Lajos.

With the heavy rain, it was impossible to use the lyre as a guide, so they maneuvered as quickly as they could, both taking a different end of Jeno. He was slippery, and they couldn't risk dropping anyone again. Once they were back in Hector's basement, they set him down near Nikita. Gertie dried him off with one of the towels and rearranged the blanket to cover them both.

When they returned for Lajos, the rains had lessened, so they once again used the lyre as their guide. It was then that Gertie realized why the gods had sent the rains: they had put out the fires. Athens was no longer in flames.

But without the deluge of rainfall, they once again had visibility. This meant Medusa could turn them to stone if they caught a glimpse of her directly. How could they carry their friend and use the lyre at the same time?

"I know," Gertie said. "We'll do what the bats do."

"Huh?"

"Echolocation."

"How?"

"You sing, and I'll navigate."

"Have you done this before?" Hector asked.

"No, but I know I can, especially now that it's stopped raining."

"What should I sing?"

They hovered in the night sky with their eyes closed, holding the statue of Lajos between them. Gertie wondered what the gods must think, if any were paying attention.

"Anything. Just hurry."

He decided on the last song he had sung, "Dreamer."

It was Gertie's favorite, and his smooth voice soothed her soul, but she tried to focus less on his magnificent singing and more on the echo of it produced by nearby objects. Using this technique, she was gradually able to get them back to Hector's house safely.

Down in the basement, Gertie took the towel to Lajos and wiped him off as best she could before adjusting the blanket to cover all three of her friends. She had a flashback to the days when she was younger, alone in her room, adjusting her dolls—her imaginary friends. She reminded herself that Jeno, Nikita, and Lajos were real, and she would find a way to save them.

She tried to reach out to Jeno's mind but found absolutely nothing. She couldn't sense his life force at all, but she fought her tears, because she wouldn't still be a vampire if he was dead.

"I know you're alive," she said to them as Hector came up behind her and circled a comforting arm around her waist. "I just want you to know that we'll figure something out. I promise, guys."

Hector pulled her closer to him, enfolding her in his strong arms. She collapsed against him, allowing him to hold her completely. That's when she let the tears fall. She was so tired and frightened and angry all at once. She wanted to scream because none of this was fair or right. What were the gods thinking? Why weren't they helping their people? Why did she feel like she held the fate of Athens on her shoulders?

Hector reminded her that the gods had sent the rain.

"That's not good enough," she said.

If only the gods would tell her what to do. She'd do whatever it took to make things right—she really would. She wanted to save the vampires and the people of Athens. She wanted to help bring about a peaceful resolution. But where should she go from here?

Hector kissed her cheek and whispered, "I'm going to change into some dry clothes. Want to borrow some?"

She was still wearing the clothes she'd taken from another house. They were too big, and they hung on her like wet paper sacks. She wouldn't mind dry clothes that fit. There was nothing like a soft t-shirt, a pair of cotton shorts, and knee-high socks to make a girl feel comfortable. Hector brought her all three.

He also brought a bottle of wine.

"I was thinking maybe you could..." he hesitated. "You know, see the future."

It was a brilliant idea.

They sat side by side on one of the couches. Then they each took a small sip from the bottle.

"Why are *you* drinking?" she asked. "Expecting to see the future, too?"

"I'm just thirsty," he said. "And my mom..." He stopped suddenly. His face went white.

A check on his thoughts revealed that, for a split second, he'd forgotten his mother had died.

"I'm sorry," Gertie said. She brushed her lips against his cheeks, his forehead, his chin. She wanted to kiss away his sad and lost expression,

"No, it's okay. I was just going to say that my mom used to let me have a little wine every once in a while."

She didn't want to read his thoughts of longing for his mother, of the grief, of the missing her so much. Gertie tried not to hear them, but they poured from Hector's mind like a waterfall. She noticed tears forming in his eyes.

"I miss her so much," he said. "And I regret what I said about her never being there for me. She was there when it mattered. And she was the only one there when I was young."

Gertie smoothed his hair away from his face. "She knew how much you loved her."

"Today wasn't the first time I forgot," he said.

"It's okay. It's pretty normal, I think."

"It is?"

She nodded. "Cheers," she said before taking a sip. Then she passed the bottle to him.

He cleared his throat. "So, while we're waiting on your prophetic vision…"

"I may not have one," she said.

"Anyway," he said. "Tell me what you found out, about your mother."

She told him what Iris had revealed. She shared her sadness over never having had the chance to meet her biological mother, Philomena, and of not knowing that her grandmother was actually a goddess. "I can't believe she lied to me."

"It was probably to protect you," he said.

"That doesn't make it right."

"If Gaia is your grandmother, then you might have some other hidden talent—besides the ability to see the future."

"Well, I have absolutely no idea what it could be. I'm not even sure this wine is doing anything but making me very sleepy."

"I'm sleepy, too."

"You haven't slept in days," she said. "And it's almost morning."

"Neither have you."

"I don't need as much sleep."

He tilted his head back, resting it on the back of the couch, exposing his throat. She could see the tramp stamp—the mark she had made on him earlier.

"Take another drink, if you need to," he said. He meant of his blood.

"I'm okay." She licked her lips. Even more than the blood, she just wanted to kiss him.

"I'm happy to oblige," he said with a twinkle in his eyes.

She couldn't with their friends right there in the room with them. It was creepy. They might be able to hear everything.

"Jeno hears everything anyway," Hector pointed out.

Then he kissed her, without waiting for permission. She didn't stop him.

That's when the vision came (of course—it couldn't wait until *after* they had had a proper make out session). She was spinning, spinning, spinning—like when she was a little girl in her backyard, playing helicopter.

Now she was running along the shoreline of a raging sea. Below her, monsters reared up from the waters. Above her was lightning. More monsters were yelling at her from the hilltop. They were Cyclopes. In her hand was the white cue billiards ball. Her father, Dionysus, threw a billiards stick, and it went through her heart, and turned her into a bull, but she kept running with the cue ball in her mouth. And she didn't know why she was running along the sea, or where she was running to, or what she was running from; she only knew that she could not drop the ball, or everyone would die.

Because the vampire virus was still in his blood, Hector had been able to see the whole thing through her eyes. "What do you think it means?"

She closed her eyes again and sighed, "I wish I had a clue."

Sometime later, she realized she had fallen asleep. Hector was snoring beside her with an arm thrown around her waist. Birds were chirping outside. Sunlight spilled in through a small window at the top of the back wall.

Wait, sunlight?

She leapt up and flew to the window with one of the couch cushions to block the light coming in. She panted as she hovered near the ceiling. Glancing at the statues in the corner, she was relieved to find Jeno still intact and well-covered by the blanket.

Then she realized she'd been in the sunlight and hadn't felt pain.

What the heck?

Her head hurt from the wine—she'd only slept a few hours, so she was sure it must still be in her system. But other than the headache, she felt no pain.

Trembling, she moved the cushion just a tiny bit to one side to let a small ray of sunshine touch her skin.

Nothing. Wasn't she still a vampire? She had to be. She was hovering in the air, for crying out loud. So why wasn't the sun painful to her?

Just then a loud sound startled her, and she dropped the couch cushion. The light poured in. She looked over at Jeno, thankful he was in a darkened corner covered by the blanket. The sound came again. It was a ringing sound. A telephone.

Hector sat up and opened his eyes. "Can you answer that?"

She looked around. "Where is it?"

He got up and pulled the phone from its cradle. "Hello?"

Gertie listened in on the conversation. It was Babá.

"Are Nikita and Klaus with you?" he asked.

"Nikita is." Hector shot a worried look at Gertie, who was still hovering near the window at the top of the back wall.

"Why haven't you come back to us?"

"I had to fight, Kirios. I'm sorry." Hector rubbed his eyes, thinking, *You have no idea.* "We'll come there as soon as we can."

"I need you to come *now*," Babá said. "Right away. Drop what you're doing. All of you."

"Has something happened?"

"Are you sure Klaus isn't with you?" Babá asked.

"We left him inside the coffin for safe keeping," Hector said.

"Tonight, when we came back from having dinner—Diane insisted that we go to her favorite restaurant even though none of us could eat. We've been so worried."

"Kirios, what happened?" Hector interrupted.

"The coffin is open, and Klaus is gone," Babá said. "He must have escaped. So, you have to ask Jeno to help you find him. Please, Hector. Will you come now? It's already nighttime here. Is the sun up there yet?"

Hector and Gertie both gasped at the same time. How was this possible?

"Hector?" Babá asked on the phone.

"Yes, Kirios Angelis," he said. "We'll figure something out and come as soon as possible."

"We'll wait up for you."

"See you soon." Hector hung up the phone and just sat there, dumbfounded.

"What could have happened to Klaus?" Gertie asked.

"I don't know," Hector replied. "Do you think Hades went ahead and gave him back his soul?"

"Maybe that's it!" she said, filling with hope. "But then why would Klaus run away? Why wouldn't he tell his parents where he was going?"

"Maybe he went looking for us."

"Do you think he went to The Vulture?" Her head was spinning with worry now. So many things could go wrong, even if Klaus had been restored. He wouldn't be a vampire, because his maker was dead. But that made him even more vulnerable.

"What's the Vulture?" Hector asked.

"That bar, where Ares killed him."

"I doubt it. And if Hades gave him his soul back, that still doesn't explain how he could have broken the chains. Jeno and I secured them before we left."

"I guess we'll go back at dusk to check around, unless you want to stay here while I go alone."

"Haven't you noticed?" she asked him, pointing to the window.

Hector frowned, and the next thing he did was rush over and inspect the statue of Jeno.

"I'm still a vampire," she said. "So Jeno must be okay."

"Then how…"

"Do you think it could be the wine?" she asked. "It's the only thing I've done differently."

Hector shrugged. "Maybe. But it seems awfully coincidental that you can tolerate the sun at the precise moment when Kirios Angelis wants us back in New York."

"What? You think it's a trap?"

"I think we need to be ready for anything," Hector said.

"Well, I'll take the rest of the bottle along, just in case."

"So we're going to New York? Now?"

"I don't think we have a choice."

"And what are we going to tell them?"

Gertie landed on her feet. "The truth."

CHAPTER SEVENTEEN

Diane's Story

It was one in the morning, New York time, when Hector and Gertie arrived at her home on Staten Island. Everybody—including Phoebe—was still awake, anxious, and waiting. The first thing they wanted to know when Gertie and Hector walked through the door was why Nikita and Jeno weren't with them.

"We need to talk," Gertie said. "Can we please all sit down in the living room? This is going to be difficult."

No one moved from the foyer. Instead, they huddled together, bracing themselves for the worst.

Mamá took Gertie's hands and squeezed them. "It's bad news. I can see it on your face. Please don't tell me my Nikita and Klausaki are gone. I beg you, Gertoula."

Phoebe clung to her mother's arm. "Mamá, I'm scared."

"They aren't gone." Hector gripped the straps of his backpack. "But they're in danger."

"How?" Babá asked.

"Oh, this is all my fault," Diane murmured.

"Let's sit down in the living room," Gertie said again.

She pushed through the huddle at the foyer and sat down on one of the couches in the main room. The coffin that had held Klaus was still there, open, the chains strewn about like snakes. Hector removed his backpack—that's where they'd put Apollo's lyre and the bottle of wine—and sat beside her. The others followed.

Gertie could read the fearful thoughts of everyone in the room, though she tried to tune them out. "First, Klaus. We think he's okay."

"Think?" Mamá asked.

"Hades told us we could have him back if we returned the helm, which we did," Hector clarified.

Babá's eyes got so wide that they were in danger of popping from their sockets. "*Hades?* Klaus was in *Hades?*"

"He may still be," Gertie said. "We were surprised when you said he'd escaped."

Mamá had turned pale. She fanned herself with a magazine from the coffee table as tears ran down her cheeks. "How will we find him? You don't even know where he is? He could be dead. He could be alive. No one knows. I think I'm going to faint."

"The goddess may have taken Klaus," Diane said.

Everyone stared at Diane with shock on their faces.

Gertie's throat tightened. "What goddess?"

Diane broke into tears. "I have so much to tell you, Gertrude. And it's not going to be easy."

"It's okay, Mom. Just tell us about the goddess you think may have taken Klaus. Is she the one who said she was my grandmother?"

Diane's face turned deathly white as she nodded. "She was here, before we went to dinner. That's why I wanted us to go out. I caught a glimpse of her upstairs. When we returned, she was gone, and so was Klaus." Then she asked Gertie, "How long have you known?"

"Since yesterday."

Hector took Gertie's hand in his and gave it a reassuring squeeze. "This sounds like good news."

"What makes you think so?" Gertie asked.

"The goddess is probably helping Klaus. And I think I know how to find her," Hector said. "The Oracle of Delphi is the omphalos of Gaia. It's where Zeus always goes when he needs to talk to her."

Mamá dropped the magazine she'd been using to fan herself and clapped her hands. "Oh, Hector, thank you! Finally, some good news!"

Babá put an arm around his wife. "What about Nikita?"

Gertie and Hector exchanged glances, both trying to figure out the best way to explain what had happened.

Mamá started crying again. "Please, just say it!"

Phoebe gripped her mother's arm.

"Hades unleashed Medusa on Athens," Hector said.

Gertie averted her eyes. "Almost the entire city has been turned to stone."

"What?" Babá jumped to his feet. "Turned to stone? Our Nikita, too? Thee moy!" He gripped his chest. For a horrifying moment, Gertie thought he was having a heart attack, but he paced around, agitated, before he returned to his seat beside Mamá.

Mamá was speechless and looked as though she, too, had been turned to stone.

"They aren't dead," Hector said. "We know they aren't dead."

"How?" Babá asked. "How can you know this?"

"I'm still a vampire," Gertie said. "So Jeno must still be alive."

"And he was also turned to stone?" Diane asked.

"Yes," Hector said. "We put him and Nikita and our friend Lajos in my basement. They're safe. Gertie and I are going to go ask Hades what to do next. He's helping us." In his mind, he added, *We think.*

"Why would Hades do such a thing?" Mamá asked.

"Sshh, Marta," Babá warned. "It's not our place to question the gods."

"Yes, it *is*," she insisted.

"I think he did it to stop the vampire uprising from getting worse," Gertie said.

"He may even be trying to save lives," Hector added. "At first, we didn't know what to think, but when we realized the people Medusa was turning into stone were still alive, well, it occurred to us that Hades was maybe freezing everything so that he could step in and take over at some point."

"When?" Mamá asked. "And how?"

Gertie stood up. "We're going to find out."

"Now?" Diane asked. "You just got home. And I have something to say to you, in private."

"But our children's lives are at stake," Mamá objected. "Please! Let them go!"

"I already know what you're going to say," Gertie told her mother. "A goddess told me everything."

Diane's mouth dropped open. "She couldn't have told you everything. What did she say? I'm not sure I would trust her, if I were you, Gertie."

"It wasn't my grandmother. It was Iris, the rainbow goddess. She told me that Gaia is my grandmother and Dionysus is my father. She said she disguised herself as a man and seduced you, and then made promises to you if you would give me back before my eighteenth birthday."

"I didn't want to give you back." Diane's face was whiter than Gertie had ever seen it. "I wasn't supposed to love you as my own, and I tried not to, but…" She covered her face and dropped off in a spasm of sobs.

Gertie had never seen her mother like this and wasn't sure what to do. Should she hug her? Give her space? Gertie stood there, frozen with shock and indecision. Her mother didn't want to give her back? Gertie had always felt like Diane couldn't wait to get rid of her.

Mamá crossed the room and knelt beside her friend, draping a thin arm across Diane's shoulders. "I can only imagine. Why didn't you tell me?"

"The goddess made me swear to tell no one," Diane said. "I didn't even tell my husband."

"Does Dad think I'm his?" Gertie asked in surprise.

Diane shook her head. "He knew I was pregnant when he married me. But he's always thought your biological father was just some man I met in Greece. He's never known the truth. In fact, I told him I was sending you to live with your father."

So they had no intention of bringing her back after her study abroad?

"If you didn't want to give me back, why did you?" Gertie was trembling now and fighting tears. "I mean, you didn't even walk me to the boat. You stayed in the limo and let your driver do it."

"I gave you back because of the goddess," Diane said. "I've always been afraid of her. That's why I never went upstairs. I hated her, always taking you from me. Every time we would begin to grow close, she would interfere. She reminded me again and again that you didn't belong to me, and that I had already benefited from the arrangement by having the wealthiest man in the world as my husband. She reminded me of all the gifts she had given us, the protection over the years. James should have been killed in a car crash years ago, but the goddess saved him." Diane struggled with her tears for a moment, before she added, "And now he wants a divorce, because he doesn't understand what I'm going through. He has no clue about all of this. He's living a new life in Venice without me, without us. The goddess probably sent him away, because I sent her away."

"You sent her away?" Gertie asked.

Diane nodded. "After we made the arrangements for you to go to Greece, I told her I'd kept my end of the bargain and was sending you back, so there was no reason for her to stay. In fact, I told her that I wouldn't put you on the ship if she didn't leave my house at once. I arranged for a funeral—that's why the casket remained closed, because no one was in it. Then everything went downhill from there." Diane wiped her eyes and added, "And I stayed in the limo that day you got on the ship in Venice because I was falling to pieces, and I didn't want you to know."

Gertie had never seen her mother such a crumpled up mess before—so vulnerable, so hurt, so destroyed. She crossed the room to Diane and knelt on the rug beside Mamá. She took Diane's hand in hers, unable to stop her tears from sliding down her cheeks. As sorry as she was for everything that had happened, she felt amazing joy in her heart to know that her mother had loved her.

The tears spilled uncontrollably down Gertie's face and she cried hard, racking sobs that shook her whole body. Her mother cupped Gertie's head in her hands and cried with her.

It was so hard to believe this wasn't a dream. Her mother *loved* her. Her mother truly *loved* her.

When she could, Gertie kissed Diane's hand. "None of this is your fault."

Diane choked out, "I shouldn't have threatened the goddess."

"You did what you were asked to do," Gertie said. "You tried your best, Mom. That's what matters."

"I'm sorry we haven't been closer," Diane said through tears. "But I want you to know that I loved you from day one. The moment I knew I was carrying you, I loved you. And I know I wasn't supposed to think of you as mine, but I did. I never saw you as anything else but my daughter. I would have fought harder for you, but I was too afraid of the goddess. I didn't care what she did to me. I worried she would take you away, and that I'd never see you again, to punish me. I even pretended to care less so she wouldn't use you against me."

"Oh, Mom," Gertie mumbled, full of confused emotions. She had always loved her grandmother so much and didn't like hearing about this side of her, and yet she was pained to hear of her mother's suffering and wanted to comfort her.

Diane slipped from the wingback chair, knelt on the rug, and threw her arms around Gertie. Gertie couldn't recall ever being held so tightly, so fiercely by her mother. She broke into more tears and turned to mush. She never wanted to leave her mother's arms again.

CHAPTER EIGHTEEN

The Oracle of Delphi

Gertie pulled Hector a little closer as she carried him across the nighttime sky from New York. The city lights twinkled below.

At two in the morning, there was still a lot going on at Staten Island and the surrounding areas.

Gertie supposed she'd never really been a part of this city. She'd always had her nose stuck in a book—which she rather missed about herself right now. She was ready to risk her life fighting for Athens, but the place she had lived all her life had no real meaning for her.

In another moment, they were above the Atlantic, which was dark and quiet compared to the city.

It had been hard to say goodbye to Mamá and Babá and Phoebe, but it had been especially hard to say goodbye to Diane. Gertie had been shocked by her mother's true feelings and had wanted to spend more time with her. Hopefully, there would be time later. Hopefully.

Right now, she had to think about Jeno, Nikita, Klaus, and Lajos—not to mention the entire city of Athens.

Yet, knowing that her mother truly loved her felt amazing. Gertie was endowed with newfound confidence. She hadn't realized just how much her self-confidence was lacking until now. Was that why she had needed the love of two boys?

Blood rushed to her face at the idea of Hector overhearing her thoughts. Remembering he no longer had the virus running through his veins, she sighed with relief.

"What?" he asked.

"Nothing."

He used his finger to brush some of her hair out of her eyes and mouth. "Better?"

She gave him a smile.

"You're so pretty, you know."

"Stop."

"It's true."

"Well, so are you."

"I know it." He winked.

She laughed and shook her head. Holding him in her arms—being so close to him for an extended period of time—felt amazing. Too bad they couldn't take their time and enjoy the flight together.

Before they'd left Gertie's house, Hector had told everyone what he knew about the Oracle of Delphi. His mother had gone many times throughout her life and had once taken him. The oracle, put in place centuries ago by Apollo, was an old priestess who always appointed a new oracle—another old priestess—when she was on her deathbed. She generally appeared at Apollo's temple on Mount Parnassus.

Hector thought they should go there, first, before finding a way to the Underworld, to see if Gaia could be summoned and, if so, to see if she knew anything about Klaus. It was, after all, where Zeus went to speak with her. And maybe the goddess would help them.

Wow. Gertie and Zeus shared the same grandmother. Wicked weird.

She was nervous about the possibility of seeing Gaia. She had such mixed emotions churning through her. On the one hand, she loved her and missed her so terribly. On the other hand, she resented Gaia for lying to her and for manipulating Diane. Gertie wasn't sure how she would feel or what she would say if she could actually be in the presence of her grandmother again. But she had to find out if Gaia had Klaus, or if she knew where he was.

As they crossed the Atlantic toward the east, the sun became visible. Gertie immediately felt the burn.

"What are we doing?" Hector shouted with alarm as they fell toward the water.

"It hurts."

They plunged in, and Gertie lay in the depths of the sea, recovering, as a school of colorful fish scattered in all directions away from her.

Hector swam to the surface for a bite of air. Then he submerged, grabbed Gertie's hand, and towed her toward the nearest island.

"I can't take it," Gertie said as they came up to a sand bar a half mile from the shore. "It's too painful." She lay back in the water like a fish. The truth was she was sick of water. She was tired of being wet. The alternative was much worse, though.

"Just take a sip of wine for me, okay? Let's see if it helps."

The sight of his wet lashes outlining his crystal blue eyes had helped her some already.

He rummaged through his pack for the bottle, opened it, and then handed it to her. She surfaced and swallowed a few gulps. The relief was instant.

She wondered if the effect of the wine came from a demigod power she possessed or from her father, helping her. She doubted her father was helping her and wondered why he had even bothered to save her life when Vladimir and the other vampires had wanted to execute her. Dionysus didn't seem to care one bit for Gertie.

At least she had her mother's love.

They set off again for Delphi. They were dry again before Europe came into view. Once they had passed Italy, Hector pointed her in the direction of Mount Parnassus. The mountains in the area were breathtaking. The rock sparkled like diamonds in the light of Helios.

When they landed on the mountain slope to the west of the little town, Gertie asked, "So why is the oracle always an old woman? Why not a man? Or a *young* woman? It seems like in every story I ever read, it's always been this crazy old woman. It seems so…cliché."

Hector led her toward the tall columns that his mind indicated were part of Apollo's temple. "The original oracle *was* a young woman, but after she was stolen and raped, Apollo appointed an old woman to take her place, and that's been the tradition ever since."

"Oh." She supposed she could deal with the cliché.

The grounds were magnificent. When they reached the top of the hill, she saw a stadium cut into the slope. Other ruins surrounded them, but it was Apollo's temple they needed.

There were no other people around yet. The sun had just risen, so it was too early for the tourists, though they would be coming soon. Gertie and Hector had to be quick.

"My mom always gave some kind of offering," Hector said as he took out Apollo's lyre from the backpack. "All I have is my song."

As anxious as she was feeling, Gertie was immediately soothed by the sound of Hector's voice singing her favorite song, "Dreamer" (to hear Hector's song, click here: https://soundcloud.com/travispohler/dreamer):

Before you close your eyes,
After you shut the door and you turn out the lights,
Remember all the days gone to waste.
Let 'em go, your shoulders know sleep's your only break.
And stay a dreamer, every day.
Dream every moment you're awake.
You may feel so far from space,
But someday the stars will remember your name.

Before you accept your fate,
After you got a job and your dreams are far too late,
Remember all the days gone to waste.
Don't hesitate, surely your job can wait, live for today.

And stay a dreamer, every day.
Dream every second you're awake.
Money will mean nothing in the grave.
You'll die no matter how much you're paid.

Dreamer,
The ground's so far beneath you.
Dreamer,
Someday they'll believe you.

Suddenly she had this thought: The problem wasn't the faith of *people* in their gods. The problem was that the *gods* didn't seem to have faith in their people.

If the gods believed in their people, they would communicate with them more efficiently.

"We need a sign," Gertie murmured.

"Maybe we're too early for her," Hector said. "My mom always came at night."

"Do you think if we prayed to Apollo, that he'd come?" Gertie asked. "This is his temple, and we have his lyre."

"I don't know. He always spoke to my mom through the oracle."

Why couldn't the gods just come out and tell her and Hector what to do?

Feeling frustrated, Gertie paced around the ruins of Apollo's temple, fighting the urge to knock something over, fighting the need to scream. Klaus could be dead, the people of Athens were a bunch of rocks, and the gods needed to do something.

"Come on, already!" she hollered to the sky. "I'm trying to help you! Why can't you help me help you?"

A loud roar shook the ground.

"Uh-oh," Gertie muttered. She'd meant to stir them into action, not piss them off.

Smoke began to rise about halfway down the hill from the temple, from a big black misshapen rock.

"That's the Sybil rock," Hector whispered. "Come on."

He took Gertie's hand, and together, they made their way toward the earth-shaking sound and smoke. When they were standing before it, Gertie could make out a green sheen in the middle of the smoke coming from the black rock. It was the image of an old woman with her hands folded. She was sitting on a tripod, and although her eyes were open, she didn't seem to actually *see* them.

"Look up into the sky, into the sky do not," the old woman said in a crackly voice. "Go to the shadow of where two birds cross, where two birds do not cross. There lies Gaia, waiting for you, not Gaia."

The image of the old woman vanished. A moment later, the black smoke thinned and the ground stopped shaking. The mountainside was quiet, except for the insects, the birds, and Gertie and Hector's breathing.

"Where two birds cross?" Hector repeated. "The shadow of where two birds cross."

"Or do not cross." She groaned.

At least they had *something* to work with.

They looked up. Two vultures were circling a cliff about a hundred yards up the mountain.

"Do you think that's the way?" Gertie asked.

"Let's go check it out."

They decided to climb rather than fly their way up. The morning was cool, but not too cold, and the sun felt amazing. Gertie would have loved the hike at any other time in her life.

Right now, the prospect of seeing her grandmother made her heart go crazy in her chest.

The circling birds crossed paths only once before flying away from Gertie and Hector as they neared the mouth of a cave.

"Grandma?" Gertie called from the outside.

"In here."

The voice didn't sound like her grandmother. It sounded like…

"Klaus?"

Gertie and Hector entered the cave. Lying on the ground looking deathly ill was Klaus.

"No, not Klaus. I am Gaia. I possessed the body of your friend to preserve it."

"Huh?" Hector took a step back.

Klaus/Gaia slowly climbed to his/her feet. "I made a deal with Hades on your behalf."

"You what?" Gertie stammered. "How? What is it?"

"Hades will return the soul of your friend to his body if you fetch the eye of Polyphemus."

Gertie blinked. She knew who Polyphemus was—the Cyclops, son of Poseidon. He was the one who had eaten Odysseus's men after the Trojan War. Odysseus had barely managed to escape himself.

Gertie knew why Hades wanted the cannibal's eye. She remembered reading about it in another story. When a person held the eye while saying ancient words, he or she could reverse Medusa's curse.

"He wants to save the people," Gertie whispered. "We were right. Hades wants to stop the war and save the people!"

"How do we get Polyphemus's eye?" Hector asked.

Gertie turned to him. "Every morning, he leaves his cave and goes to the sea to wash it."

"How do you know that?" Hector asked.

"I read a lot, remember?"

"Right. Do you also know how to find Cyclopes Island?"

Gertie turned to Gaia/Klaus. "No, I don't. Do you?"

"It's west of here," Gaia said. "In the Ionian Sea near the toe of the boot of Italy."

Gertie knew what else lived in that area. "Scylla and Charybdis," she murmured. "Aren't those monsters around there, too?"

"How do you know *that?*" Hector asked. "Wait. Don't tell me. I know. You read a lot."

"And who do you think fostered her love of the ancient Greek stories?" Gaia asked.

Gertie rubbed her eyes. Looking at the body of Klaus made it difficult for her to imagine the kind and loving woman who had raised her. And now she wondered if the kindness and love had been part of an act. Maybe the goddess was just using Gertie in her plan to get Iris back from Hera. Diane had felt manipulated by and even frightened of Gaia. Maybe she wasn't the loving grandmother Gertie so desperately missed.

Klaus's body began to shimmer and glow. Then it shook fiercely, as though in a fit of epilepsy.

In the next instant, Klaus dropped toward the floor, though Hector caught him before he hit the ground. Shimmering beside the body of Klaus was the woman Gertie had always thought of as her grandmother.

"Is that really you?" Gertie asked uncertainly through a very tight, dry throat. It was a shock to see this woman. For months, Gertie had thought she was dead. A part of Gertie longed to throw her arms around the woman who had been her only comfort growing up; and yet another part of her was wary. Who really was she? Friend or foe?

"Oh, my sweet Gertrude," Gaia said with a frown. "It saddens me to know you doubt my love for you. I have always loved you as if you were my own daughter."

"Diane said you were mean and manipulative to her. How could you love me and be so cruel to her?"

"I was trying to protect her," Gaia said. "I knew that if you were to have any chance of being the one, you'd eventually return to Greece."

"Kids leave home all the time," Gertie pointed out.

Gaia sighed. "Perhaps I was a little jealous. You didn't belong to her."

"I don't belong to anyone," Gertie said. "I'm my own person."

"I can see that. You've become strong and independent. I'm proud of you, even if you are a vampire."

Gertie hated it when people said, "Even if you are a vampire." It was like saying "even if you are a girl," or "even if you are an American." It wasn't a very nice thing to say.

"Why didn't you tell me the truth about my parents? Why did you lie to me?"

"You already know the answer to that. As Iris said, the more we interfere with our destinies, the crueler the Fates prove to be."

"I trusted you." Gertie fought back tears and found it hard to breathe.

"With good reason. I protected you from every danger."

"Except this war," Gertie said. "You let me become a vampire—not that there's anything wrong with being one." She was only fooling herself. She longed to be human again.

"It seemed like an important part of your destiny."

Blood rushed to Gertie's face. "I have no idea how to get Iris back for you. I hate to disappoint you, but I don't think I'm the one."

"You either are or you aren't. Whether you believe it to be true has no bearing."

Would Gaia stop loving her if Gertie wasn't the one in the prophecy?

"Never," Gaia said. "I would never stop loving you. And I will do everything in my power to help you in ways that might go unnoticed by the Fates. Now, can I please have a hug before I have to jump back into the body of your friend?"

Gertie hesitated, but as soon as the memories of their story time, their long conversations, and their walks together in the neighborhood swept through Gertie's mind, she couldn't resist rushing into Gaia's arms. Tears flowed down her cheeks. This was the only person she'd ever had a strong connection with. She couldn't pretend otherwise. She needed Gaia's love to continue, even though she also had Diane's.

Gaia kissed the top of Gertie's head and then vanished. Hector was startled when "Klaus" came to.

"His body is weakening every day," Gaia said inside the body of Klaus. "That's why I'm stuck here in this cave. My powers are diminished through this possession; otherwise, I would get the eye from the Cyclops myself."

"Are you saying that Klaus could die if we don't hurry?" Hector asked.

"Yes," Gaia said. "The human body begins to break down in the absence of its soul. I'm doing my best to preserve it, but I can only do so much."

"What do we do with the eye once we get it?" Hector asked.

"Return here, and we'll go to Hades together."

"Thank you for helping," Gertie said. "I've missed you so much."

"As I have you, my darling."

Hector turned to Gertie. "Ready to go?"

She wanted to say, yes, she was ready for anything, but she was tired and emotional after all that she'd discovered about her past. She wished she had time to just sit somewhere and process it all. She wasn't ready to sneak past Scylla and Charybdis on the way to Cyclopes Island. She wasn't ready to face a cannibal and attempt to steal his eye. She wasn't ready for any of the things the gods expected her to do, but, nevertheless, she would try.

"Let's go," she said.

CHAPTER NINETEEN

The Straight of Messina

As they descended the mountain by foot, Hector turned to Gertie. "How will we know the island when we find it?"

"From what I've read, there's a big cave overlooking the beach, where Polyphemus lives."

"I've heard of his cave."

"And then just beyond that, there's an orchard of fruit trees—fig, pomegranate, apple. I can't remember them all."

"Man, I'm hungry."

"Then past the orchard are rolling grassy hills where all the sheep graze during the day. I think there are also big cheeses laid out and lots of buckets of milk."

"A cheeseburger, American style, sounds really good right now."

She giggled. He was so cute, even during a crisis. "And I think there's a little village in the very center, where other Cyclopes live. There's a tavern, I think. Somewhere, there's a forge—next door to the tavern—where they make Zeus's thunderbolts. But I don't think there's a cheeseburger stand."

Hector grinned. "You describe it as though you've been there."

"Hey. Books take you places." Then she added, "That should be on a t-shirt."

He laughed. "If it isn't already."

Gertie stopped in her tracks. "My vision! It was about getting the eye!"

Hector snapped his fingers. "That's right! There were Cyclopes!"

"I was carrying the white cue ball, remember?"

"Yeah. What do you think that means?" He continued down the hill, so she followed.

"Do you think I should get one and take it with us? Maybe I'm supposed to put the cue ball, I don't know, in Polyphemus's socket, or something, when we take out his eye." She shuddered, wondering how disgusting it would be.

"I thought you said we'd grab it after he's already taken it out to wash it."

"He may have already done that this morning. We might have missed that opportunity."

As they neared Apollo's temple and the other ruins, Hector shook his head. "I don't see how we're going to get close enough to take out the eye."

"He's a shepherd, right?"

"So?"

"Maybe he naps while the sheep graze."

"And if he never goes to sleep?" Hector asked.

"You'll lull him by playing the lyre."

He grinned and kissed the side of her face. "Have I told you how smart you are?"

She tipped her head back and laughed. "You know what else we have to be happy about?"

"Yes, I do. No one has to trade a soul for Klaus."

She clapped her hand to her chest. "I'm so relieved about that."

"Me, too. I've been afraid that no matter how much I begged, Hades would choose *you*." Hector stopped hiking, grabbed her by the waist, and pulled her up against him. "I hope you know by now that I want to be with you."

Her heart drummed wildly against her ribs. "But I'm a vampire."

"I don't care. Do you?"

She frowned.

"I can't read your mind," he said. "Are you worried about me growing old? Is that it? You don't want to be with someone who'll turn old and gray while you stay young and beautiful?"

She laid her hand against his cheek. "No. God, how can you think that?"

He studied her face. "Then what?"

"I'm scared…of having to go on without you."

Tears flooded his eyes, which surprised her. Jeno had often cried, but not Hector. And, even now, he wasn't actually crying. Moist eyes meant a big reaction for Hector, though.

"Then turn me," he said. "We'll both be immortal."

She jerked her chin down in surprise. "I couldn't do that to you. I know how wrong it feels to you to break a law you've had to enforce. Plus, even if you could reconcile yourself with breaking it, you'd have to live in darkness, on the blood of humans. It's no easy life."

"It's my choice."

"What about the law?"

"We'll change it."

She wanted to be with him more than anything, but the idea of making him give up his humanity made her sick to her stomach. She wasn't sure she could do it. "Hector, I…"

"It's a lot for me to ask," he said sadly. "Maybe too much."

"Oh, Hector…"

He turned away. "It's okay. Come on. I know where we can get a cue ball."

They ran along the countryside, Hector leading the way. She stared at his back, barely noticing the landscape around them, feeling like he was running away from her and his feelings for her, like he'd decided he had to let her go. It was the same conclusion Jeno had come to. Maybe Gertie would end up alone.

Her chest felt very tight, but she kept on running.

The town of Delphi was spooky quiet, like the way ghost towns were always portrayed in the movies. Gertie's heart sank in her chest when it dawned on her that maybe Medusa had been here, too. Dust covered everything—the abandoned vehicles and buildings. Unlike Athens, there were no people here turned to stone and no signs of devastation by fire. It looked as though the town had been evacuated.

"What happened here?"

"Maybe they heard about Medusa in Athens. Maybe they left the country."

"Or maybe they've all been turned to vampires."

Gertie followed Hector down the street to a place called Hotel Zeus and then flinched when something came around the corner.

She sighed with relief when she saw it was only a cat.

"Poor little thing," Hector said, scooping it up. "It must be hungry and thirsty."

Without looking back at Gertie, Hector carried the cat into the hotel. Like the rest of the city, the building seemed abandoned. Gertie followed Hector through a lobby into a pub. Hector went to the kitchen in back and filled a bowl with water from the faucet. Then he rummaged around for snacks and found a box of jerky. He ate some himself and put the rest in a bowl on the floor for the cat.

Gertie watched him petting the cat. She was searching for the right words to say—had been searching the entire time they'd been running.

She still didn't know what she was going to say, but she had to say something. "Hector, I…"

He stood up from where he'd been kneeling with the cat. "This can't be about you or me right now. Right now, we have to think about Greece."

She looked down at the cat and nodded. "You're right."

"Let's grab the cue ball and go."

Hector found a rag from the kitchen and wrapped it around the white cue ball from the pool table. He didn't want the ball to knock around and crack the bottle of wine. While he had it out, Gertie took another sip of wine, to protect herself from the sun. She offered to carry Hector if he wanted to fly, but he said he needed to run.

"It'll take about the same amount of time, either way," he said.

"But we can fly in a bee-line," she said. "We won't be able to do that on land."

"I slow you down when we fly. We'll be lighter and faster on our feet."

So she followed him again all the way to Patras—nearly two hours of staring at his back. By the time they reached the port, Gertie felt that although running might be therapeutic for some people, she was more emotional than ever. The pressure of saving her friends, of saving Athens, and of sparing the hearts of the two boys she loved was weighing on her like a ton of bricks.

And now that Hector had basically given up on her, she felt physically ill.

At least there were people here. Whatever had turned Delphi into a ghost town had not yet impacted Patras. She followed Hector down the street to the docks.

For the first time, Gertie was beginning to doubt that she could do anything about the uprising. She was just a seventeen-year-old girl who couldn't even decide which boy she loved, or whether she could trust her parents and grandmother and the gods. Her only talent was the unreliable gift of visions, and it only happened after drinking wine. How had she gotten herself in this situation? Hector, and Jeno, and the Angelis family, and the city of Athens needed someone else. She wasn't meant to fight. She was meant to read. She'd lived her whole life happily behind the pages of her books.

Sort of happily.

Nausea swept over her.

"You okay?" Hector asked as they slowed to a walk.

She nodded and then wondered if she could tell him the truth. She felt like an imposter. She shouldn't be here with the likes of him. Tears pricked her eyes.

"I'm going to charter a boat," he said as he walked up to a hut near the harbor. "I think I'll be able to find my way better above water than below."

She supposed the same was true for her. Navigating underwater was no easy feat.

"You don't want to save your money and fly?"

"Not really."

She turned from him to hide the blush that raced to her cheeks. He didn't want to be in her arms. He would rather give up a chunk of money and take a boat across the sea than fly in her arms.

The sun was at high noon a half hour later when they sailed across the sea toward Italy. The water was smooth as glass and the sky was as blue as Hector's eyes. Under any other circumstances, the boat ride might have been romantic, but Gertie's stomach was tied in knots over the vast uncertainty before them.

Vast. That was the right word. The uncertainty was vast, just like the sea.

Although the captain had never heard of Cyclopes Island, except in stories, he headed in the direction of the toe of the boot of Italy. He had said he would not enter the Straight of Messina, which was the narrow passageway between the toe of Italy and the northern tip of Sicily. He would only take them to the east coast. If they wanted to search within and beyond the straight, he would drop them off and they could charter another boat. There'd been no other boat in Patras willing or able to take them, so Hector had gone ahead and chartered this one.

Later, while they were out to sea, and Hector had asked the captain why, Gertie already knew the answer, and not just because she could read the captain's mind. She'd read all about Scylla and Charybdis and the number of ships they'd overwhelmed in the Straight of Messina.

Only the most experienced seaman dared to venture in the area threatened by monsters.

"I'm being especially careful after what I heard last night," the captain said.

Hector made a visor with one hand to shield the sun and studied the captain's face. "What was that?"

"I've seen some strange things in my lifetime," he said. "But nothing as strange as what everyone was talking about at the bar last night. The rumor is that the gods are angry with Greece and are sending monsters to destroy the people."

"Monsters?" Gertie crossed her arms, nonchalantly. "What kind of monsters?"

"I'm just telling you what I heard. Some say vampires. Others say Medusa."

"Do you believe the rumors?" Hector asked.

"I believe in monsters," he said. "And I don't want to tempt fate."

They combed the sea for signs of Cyclopes Island, but all they saw was the glass-like water stretching out to the shores of Italy and Sicily. The captain took them to a port in southern Italy, where they said they would charter another boat, but as soon as the captain had headed back, they left the crowded port and headed for the beach.

They found a lonely stretch that was too rough and rocky for swimming and sunbathing.

"Swim or fly?" she asked him. "We'll be able to spot the island better in the sky."

"And we'll be less vulnerable, too," he added.

Because her skin was tingling from the sun, she took another sip of wine, and then said, playfully, "Most folks use sunscreen, but not Captain Morgan."

She'd hoped to ease the tension between them by making fun of herself, but Hector didn't even smile. A check of his mind revealed how nervous he was about having to fly in her arms. He kept reminding himself to focus on the quest. Lives were depending on him.

After she put the wine away, and Hector strapped on the backpack, she asked, "Ready?"

He nodded without looking at her.

"We need both of our eyes scanning the sea," she said. "So I should lift you from behind."

Oh, this is going to be so awkward, she thought, and she found his thoughts echoing hers.

"Then maybe you should wear the pack." He took it off and handed it to her.

Once she had the pack in place, she tucked her arms beneath his and clasped her hands together at his chest.

Gosh, he feels so good.

Again, Hector's mind echoed her with, *Man, she feels nice.*

In another moment, Gertie lifted up into the air. In order to see around him, she had no choice but to press up against him and rest her chin on his shoulder. It was so painful to hear his heart pounding and his mind reprimanding himself for the way he responded to her body. And she didn't have the strength to stop listening. She had to know how he felt, even though it hurt.

You've got to let her go, man. Keep it together.

Even though it was painful, holding him also filled her with joy. Pressed up against his strong back with her face against his shoulder, his blond hair whipping in the wind against her cheek, Gertie never wanted to leave. This was home to her. He was home to her.

Tears filled her eyes. She tightened her hold on him and tried to focus on searching for the island, but then his hands unexpectedly closed over hers at his chest, and she gasped.

"I'm trying to let you go, but it feels so wrong," he said.

"Don't."

He was quiet for a moment. "Don't what? Talk about it?"

"Don't let me go."

He turned around in her arms to face her. He searched her face. "What are you saying?"

"I love you," she said without intending to.

His eyebrows lifted.

"And I want to be with you. I don't care if I'm immortal."

"Gertie, are you sure? Are you really sure about this?"

She swallowed hard and nodded.

"But what about what you said? About having to go on without me?"

Please don't tell me this unless you really mean it, he thought.

"I'll cross that bridge when I get there," she said, and without telling him, she'd decided she could always end her life if the pain of going on without him was unbearable. Or maybe, if she couldn't bear to let him go, she'd turn him into a vampire, but only after he'd had a full life.

He stared at her a moment longer, as if making sure she had really meant it, and then he grabbed a fistful of her hair and pulled her lips to his. *I hope this isn't a dream. If it is, may I never wake up.*

His kisses filled her with happiness.

"Why are you crying?" he asked her. "Are you worried?"

She gave him a smile and shook her head. "Not anymore."

In the next instant, something wet and rope-like wrapped around her ankle and pulled her down toward the sea. Hector drew his sword just as they plunged into the depths of the straight.

Gertie struggled against the thing holding onto her ankles as Hector swung his blade through the water, trying to set her free. Bubbles swirled all around them, impairing her ability to see, since her x-ray vision didn't work underwater. Something green and slimy wrapped around her waist. Hector sliced it in two, and blood spilled into the ocean.

Even without her acute vampire hearing, which didn't work underwater, Gertie was startled by the screams coming from all six heads of Scylla. The monster's six long, serpent necks and dragon heads ended in rows and rows of sharp teeth. Twelve tentacle-like legs swung around the two teens, so that as soon as they had pried themselves free of one tentacle, there was another in its place. Around Scylla's waist grew the heads of six yelping dogs with more snapping teeth. And then there were her crab-like pincers, which she used to drag herself along the ocean floor. She was the strangest monster Gertie had ever read about, and she was even stranger in person.

Gertie's fears had come true. She and Hector had barely reached the straight, and the monster had literally grabbed them from the air. It was almost like Scylla had been waiting for them, watching for them. The monster must have known they were coming. But how?

Just then a swirling whirlpool surrounded them and added to the confusion.

Charybdis!

The white foamy monster first pulled the water toward her as she sucked in the sea, and then she hurled everything away from her, churning and churning, as she exhaled. Gertie reached out for Hector's hand, not wanting to be torn away from him. He held onto her, but a check of his mind revealed that he needed air, and he needed it soon.

Then another slimy tentacle wrapped itself around her waist and tore her hand from Hector's.

Hector focused all his concentration into remaining calm, but his need for air was winning out. Gertie strained her neck to get another glimpse of him and was startled by his eyes nearly bulging from their sockets.

He needed air!

Full of panic and sheer determination, Gertie stretched open her mouth, erected her fangs, and pierced the flesh of the slimy tentacle holding her.

Gertie didn't care that the blood tasted stale and bitter. She sucked and sucked until the monster began to weaken. Gertie gagged and nearly vomited before she finally slipped from Scylla's grasp and found Hector sinking toward the ocean floor, as lifeless as an anchor. His eyes were closed, and a check of his mind revealed that he was no longer conscious.

"Hector!" she cried into the sea.

Gertie used every bit of her vampire strength to swim to him. Scylla hung in the water, her tentacles and necks a tangled mess, but once Gertie was free of the massive beast, she grabbed Hector's arm and towed him toward the surface just as Charybdis drew the sea toward her again in a giant whirlpool.

No longer as still as glass, the surface of the sea churned with swells as huge as mountains. Gertie struggled to keep Hector's face above water, but Charybdis was furious and unrelenting.

"Hector?" Gertie cried, struggling to keep him afloat. "Hector, please wake up!"

The backpack containing Apollo's lyre, the cue ball, and the wine, was awkward on her back in the virulent waves, and she was tempted to let it loose. She clenched her teeth and prayed to all of the gods she knew to please, please help Hector. She reminded them that he'd been trying to save Athens and to help the gods and the vampires.

"He's an exceptional person!" she shouted above the water as warm tears filled her eyes. "He doesn't deserve this! Please!"

If the gods allowed Hector to die, she would never again have another thing to do with them, because it just wasn't right to allow one of *their* warriors, one of *their* servants, who had served so well, to die like this.

Using her vampire senses above water, she listened for a heartbeat in Hector's chest and found none.

"No!" she screamed.

Tears poured down her cheeks, and she knew she could not live without Hector. Too much of her life had been based on lies and manipulation, but he had always been true and real. He had made her want to be a better person, he had made her want to do her part to save Athens, and he had made her want to hold on to the idea of happiness. If happiness and joy were really possible, they were only possible for her with him.

When the gods appeared to do nothing, Gertie decided to take matters into her own hands. The only thing she could think to do was to animate Hector with the vampire virus. She stretched open her mouth, and, even though she still felt sick from the blood of Scylla, she erected her fangs and lifted Hector's chin to expose his neck. As she was about to penetrate his flesh, something snatched them from the water, and she and Hector were lifted up into the air, hundreds of yards from the raging sea.

Gertie looked up to see the giant white crane that had rescued them months ago flapping its magnificent wings. Hector's father had finally come to help them. She hoped and prayed he wasn't too late.

CHAPTER TWENTY

Gertie's Other Hidden Talent

Soon the giant crane released Gertie and Hector on an island beneath a row of fruit trees and landed on its feet beside them. She carefully stretched Hector's limp body out on the ground, and when the crane did nothing but stare down at her, she began giving him mouth-to-mouth resuscitation.

The next time she looked up at Hephaestus, he had transformed into a man. Beautiful, strong, with dark golden hair and beard, he knelt beside his son, took a deep breath, and then blew into Hector's mouth. Hector opened his eyes and sat up, shocked and disoriented.

Gertie threw her arms around Hector's neck and cried tears of relief.

"Father?" Hector blinked.

"Thank you!" she said to Hephaestus, relieved that a god had finally come to help them. "Oh, Hector. Are you okay?"

He blinked again. "Yeah. I think so."

Hephaestus climbed to his feet. "How dare Poseidon try to kill my son?"

"Poseidon?" Gertie's jaw dropped open. So Poseidon had sent Scylla and Charybdis? "Do you think he was trying to protect Polyphemus?"

"Maybe," Hephaestus said. "But he also fears Medusa's wrath and wants the eye for himself."

Hector, still recovering, let Gertie help him to his feet. "He would take the eye from his own son?"

"He wants to borrow it. He and Dionysus have formed an alliance to stop Hades."

"Oh, no," Gertie moaned.

"Dionysus wants to continue to reign over the vampires, and Poseidon wants Medusa's head."

"And what about Athena?" Hector asked.

"She wants Medusa's head back on her shield," Hephaestus said. "And she wants to destroy the vampires. And worse, Zeus is on her side."

Hector and Gertie exchanged looks of horror.

"Why does Athena want to destroy them?" Gertie murmured.

"They have always been a threat to her city," the god explained. "To her people."

"But Hades wants to change that," Hector pointed out.

"And Hera has pledged to help Hades. She wants the vampires to live, but only because she hopes to see them taken from Dionysus."

Gertie shook her head. Hera's hate ran deep, but at least, this time, it would benefit the right cause.

"Although the twins have decided to remain neutral, the rest of us are behind Hades, too," Hephaestus added.

"That's great!" Gertie said with wide eyes. She counted on her fingers. "That's Aphrodite and Ares and Hermes and Persephone and Demeter…"

"Not Demeter," Hephaestus said. "She's away for the winter."

"But still!" Gertie cried. "We have enough gods on our side to win this thing, right?"

"Unfortunately, there's a kink in Hades's plan," Hephaestus said. "Medusa has made it clear that she would rather have revenge on Poseidon than accept redemption. She's no longer cooperating with Hades."

"What?" Hector gasped.

"That's terrible!" Gertie wailed. "Where is she now?"

"No one knows," Hephaestus replied. "That's why Poseidon is desperate for the eye of the Cyclops. He's afraid she's going after his kingdom."

"We have to get it before he does," Gertie said. "Can you take us to Cyclopes Island?"

"I already have. You are standing on it."

Just above their heads, lightning flashed, and a chariot came into view between the clouds.

"That's Poseidon," Hephaestus said. "He's under attack by Zeus but on his way here himself."

"We've got to stop him," Hector said anxiously. "Father, what should we do?"

"Fight," Hephaestus said.

"Wait!" Gertie stretched her eyes wide and lifted a finger in the air. She was having a eureka moment. "I just realized what I have to do!"

She pulled off the backpack, unzipped it, and fished around for the cue ball. Then she gave the pack to Hector and held the ball in the air. "This is our distraction."

"What do you mean?" Hector wrinkled his brow.

"In my vision, I was running across the shoreline with this in my hand, and all the gods and monsters were chasing me."

"I know," Hector said. "I saw it, too."

"So, I'm going to run out where all can see. I'll claim to have the eye, right? And then while I have everyone distracted, you and your dad grab the real eye and take it to the Underworld."

"I can't enter the Underworld," Hephaestus said. "But I know someone who can. Let's go."

"Hold on." Hector grabbed Gertie's shoulders and pulled her in for a kiss. "I don't want to split up."

"We have to do this for Greece, and for Klaus and the others."

"I'm scared to leave you. I'm scared you'll get killed, like in your vision."

"I didn't die. I turned into a bull." She squeezed his hand. "I'm a vampire and a demigod. I'm a powerful badass. I got this, okay?"

Hector nodded. "You're right. Be careful. Protect that heart of yours. It's mine, remember?"

Gertie gave him her bravest smile. "I remember."

"Avoid the sea and sky," Hephaestus warned. "And good luck."

Hephaestus transformed back into a crane and lifted off with Hector on his back. They headed for Polyphemus, who was likely shepherding his flock in the hills. Gertie ran in the opposite direction, toward the shoreline, shouting, "Hades! I've got it! I've got the eye! Hades, come get it! I've got the eye of Polyphemus!"

As she ran along the shoreline, lightning struck at her from the sky, but her keen vampire senses helped her to dodge the attacks. A wall of water formed several yards out and crawled toward the shoreline. Gertie was sure she saw Scylla's tentacles reaching out from the top of it. At that moment, she saw her father racing toward her in the form of a golden ram. All the sheep that were grazing on the hillside scattered, braying their alarm as the ram charged down the hill toward Gertie, horns pointed and prepared to strike.

In her vision, he had thrown the billiards stick at her heart, and it had pierced through, turning her into a bull. Maybe she really had foreseen her death.

She couldn't believe her own father would want to destroy her. He cared more about ruling the vampires than he did about the welfare of his own child. If only she, too, could transform into a powerful beast, like the bull of her vision, and show her father that he couldn't discard her so easily.

As he neared her, she closed her eyes and wished she were a bull with horns as mighty as those of the golden ram.

Suddenly, she found herself running with her feet *and hands*—only they weren't hands. They were powerful hooves digging into the rock and sand. The cue ball was in her mouth. A glance toward the wall of water crawling toward her revealed her reflection. She was the bull from her vision, and she was about to clash horns with her father.

Beside the ram, a white bull appeared. For a moment, Gertie faltered. How would she fare against two horned beasts? But in the next moment, another beast appeared, running alongside her, and headed for the white bull.

"I'm Hera," the ivory ox shouted. "I will stop Poseidon."

All four beasts collided. Gertie's horns hooked with those of Dionysus, and though she used all her strength against him, he lifted her from the ground and flung her into the air. She spun once before getting her bearings and was glad she could fly, even in this form…though it all seemed like a dream.

As she searched the island for her father, hoping to fight with him again, to prove to him that he couldn't dismiss her, a bolt of lightning struck her on the back, paralyzing her. She fell through the air, her bull body quickly transforming back into her human form. The cue ball fell from her mouth, and because she was paralyzed, Gertie could do nothing to stop it.

Before she reached the sea, she landed on something hard and invisible, and as soon as she had, she found herself in the arms of Hades. He was wearing the helm, and so was invisible to all but her and to Persephone, who was standing beside him in the chariot.

"Do you have the eye?" he asked her.

She couldn't move, couldn't speak. Her eyelids closed of their own accord, and all went dark.

CHAPTER TWENTY-ONE

Gaia's Arms

Gertie opened her eyes and blinked, trying to get her bearings. The last thing she remembered was falling through the sky after being zapped by Zeus's thunderbolt.

And then Hades and Persephone had caught her in their chariot.

She hadn't been able to move or speak. Was she still paralyzed?

She blinked again, and cautiously lifted her head. It took all her strength, but she *did* move. Next, she tried lifting an arm. It felt heavy, like someone was sitting on her.

Slowly turning her head from side to side, she didn't recognize where she was. It was dark and cavernous. Emeralds, rubies, and diamonds were inlaid in the walls of the cave and sparkled with the light from a fire, casting shadows all around her. The room had the feel of a church, though it was made of rock and dirt.

She clutched what she now realized was a feather-stuffed mattress, and tried to sit up, but couldn't.

"Take it easy," came the voice of her grandmother.

"Gaia? Where am I?"

"The Underworld."

"And where are you?"

The pillow behind her moved, and a soft hand stroked her cheek. "I'm holding you, like when you were little."

Gertie strained to see her grandmother's face. Maybe she should have been frightened to awaken in the arms of a goddess, but this was her grandmother, and, instead, she felt comforted.

Gaia kissed her forehead and removed her arm from beneath Gertie's head, adjusting the pillow. Then she sat up and gazed down at Gertie. "You've been asleep for three days."

"I had the strangest dream that I'd turned into a bull." Gertie tried to rub her eyes, but she couldn't lift her hands all the way to her face.

"That wasn't a dream."

Gertie cleared her throat of the crud that had built up there while she'd been sleeping and struggled to recall what had happened before she'd passed out.

She'd really turned into a bull? "How is that possible?"

"It was a hidden talent," Gaia said. "Like your gift of prophecy. Usually only my *immortal* descendants can shift into animals. Only a very few demigods have had that gift."

"Maybe they had it and didn't know it," Gertie wondered out loud. She wouldn't have thought of transforming into a bull if it hadn't happened in her vision.

"I suppose," Gaia said. "But you should still feel very special. It's a rare gift. I'm glad it's yours."

"Why a bull? Do you know?"

"Maybe because Taurus is your astrological sign. Or because you're stubborn. I don't know, Gertrude."

"Where's Hector?"

"He's fine. You should have seen him in action, though. He is the reason you're still alive—and Klaus, too."

"Klaus is alive? Oh my gosh! What happened?"

"Hector saw you fall from the sky and disappear," Gaia said, as she stroked Gertie's hair like she used to do. "So after he and Hephaestus got the eye of the Cyclops, they flew to Iris, who helped Hector deliver it to Hades."

"Oh, thank goodness."

"But Hector refused to give it to Hades at first."

"Why?"

"He made demands. Smart boy, too, because you and he had been doing all the work for these gods, and if you ask me, they've been ungrateful."

"Thank you." Gertie smiled. "So what were Hector's demands?"

"He threatened to destroy both the eye and Apollo's lyre if Hades didn't summon Apollo and do everything in his power to find you and save your life."

"He threatened the gods?"

"Oh, yes. Sometimes it's the only way."

"But people get thrown into Tartarus for that."

"I know."

"And they listened to him? Why didn't they just kill him and take the eye and the lyre?"

"Hector had hidden them, and no one else, except maybe Hephaestus, knew where they were."

With some effort, Gertie managed a nod. "And Hector didn't know Hades was the one who had caught me?"

"Hades informed him, but Hector wasn't the least bit satisfied. He wanted you *healed*, and he wouldn't budge."

"And what did Hades do?"

"He sent the Furies for Apollo, and the god of medicine came and gave you an elixir to help you recover from the strike of the lightning bolt."

"Wow. That's amazing. So I'm going to fully recover?"

"Yes. Though, you'll always be a vampire."

As happy as she was to know she would soon have the full use of her limbs again, she was a little disappointed to hear that Apollo's elixir hadn't cured her completely by restoring her humanity. That would have been a very happy ending for her, for it would have meant she and Hector could have a family of their own.

She chastised herself for not being more grateful for her life.

The main reason she was so disappointed about being a vampire was the fact that vampires couldn't reproduce. Not everyone got to have a family. Maybe she and Hector could adopt. But could she stand watching her children grow old and die while she remained in the body of a seventeen-year-old?

"And what about Klaus?"

"Hector also threatened to destroy the eye if Hades didn't return Klaus's soul and restore your friends who'd been turned to stone by Medusa."

"So did Hades agree?"

"Yes. Klaus and his sister are back in New York in Diane's house with their parents."

Tears of relief sprang to Gertie's eyes. "Oh, I'm so glad to hear that! Mamá and Babá must be so relieved. Thank goodness."

"Thank *Hector*," Gaia said with a smile. "And *you*, of course, because he wouldn't have managed to get the real eye if you hadn't risked your life distracting the gods with your decoy."

Gertie blushed.

"You were very brave, my dear."

"And Jeno?" Gertie bit her lip. "Is Jeno okay, too?"

"Yes. Right now he's with Hector, helping with the hunt for Medusa. Lajos is with them, too."

She was relieved that both Jeno and Lajos were no longer made of stone, but she was worried that it wouldn't last—not if they were hunting Medusa. "So it's not over yet."

"No, my dear. Athena is still bent on destroying the vampires, and she, Hades, and Poseidon are in a race for Medusa's head."

"Has Hades used the eye to free the vampires who've been turned to stone?" Gertie asked.

"Not yet. But he has collected most of them and brought them here, to the Underworld, so they are safe from Athena and Zeus."

"Most of them?"

"Not all could be saved from Athena."

Gertie groaned. She wanted to tell Athena that the vampires were her people, too. The vampires of Athens were Athena's people, and she should be their protector, not their destroyer. And Gertie herself felt so conflicted and guilty that she didn't *want* to be a vampire. It was mainly because of Hector, because her heart belonged to him.

But even if she weren't in love with Hector, Gertie would still prefer to be human. The superpowers of a vampire were incredible, but the dependency on human blood and the inability to tolerate sunlight were too high a price to pay for those powers. Didn't this make her a hypocrite? She wanted the gods and demigods and humans to respect the vampires, yet she didn't want to be one. Her words and actions should be consistent. She needed to embrace her vampirism.

Maybe she should consider the idea of turning Hector. Maybe they *could* be happy together as vampires—*if* Athena didn't destroy them all.

"I wish I could be there, fighting alongside them," Gertie said. "I hate being left behind."

Gaia frowned. "I've enjoyed having you in my arms again, sweet girl."

"And I'm grateful, Grandma. I'm glad I had some time with you again. You don't know how miserable I was when you...left."

"It was Diane that forced me to go."

"I know."

"You are my sweet child, my favorite of all my grandchildren. I didn't want to leave you."

Gertie's eyes widened. She was Gaia's favorite? "But I don't think I'm the one in the prophecy. You know I would help you if I could. I just don't see how I can."

"It doesn't matter." Gaia kissed her forehead once again. "My love for you is unconditional."

A smile crossed Gertie's face as more tears fled her eyes.

"But I do think you're the one," Gaia added. "And I know how you can fulfill the prophecy."

Gertie's eyebrows lifted, and her mouth dropped open. "How?"

"Whoever has Medusa's head will control the fate of the vampires, because Athena would forfeit the war to have her trophy back. Don't you agree?"

"Yes, but what has that got to do with me? You don't expect me to…"

"I know where Medusa is," Gaia said with a grin.

Gertie felt some of the movement coming back to her limbs, and she was able to sit up. Maybe it was the shock. "Then we need to tell Hades."

"Not yet."

"I want Medusa to have another chance. She doesn't deserve to be Athena's trophy."

"Hades gave her that chance. Medusa chose revenge. If she hadn't, this war would be over, and Hades would have won. The vampires would be safe. All would be restored, except…"

"Harmony."

"The Earth needs its Harmony, dear. You must see that."

"I still don't know how I can do anything about it."

"You may not be able to, but I'm offering you an opportunity to save the vampires and restore Harmony in one brave deed."

"What?"

"It will be dangerous, and you may decide you don't want to do it. And I must admit I'm fearful of even offering you the choice."

"What choice?"

"If you can control the fate of the vampires, a deal can be struck with Hera."

Gertie stared into space. What was her grandmother asking her to do?

"Listen, Gertrude. I don't want to keep Iris all to myself. I just want her to be shared. Hera has made her a personal assistant when Harmony should belong to everyone."

"You just want to free Iris from her servitude?"

"Exactly—not to make her *my* servant, but to help her be free to do more than refill the clouds and run Hera's errands."

"So, what exactly do you want me to do? What's the choice?"

Gaia stood up and squared herself to Gertie. "I want you to know that I would do this myself if I could."

"Grandma, what are you talking about?"

"I've trapped Medusa in my kneecap."

Gertie studied her grandmother's knees.

Gaia laughed. "Not these kneecaps. In my *literal* kneecap. This body is just a projection. I am Earth, remember? My body is this entire planet."

"And where, exactly, is your kneecap?"

"Mount Everest."

Gertie gasped. "Isn't that in China?"

"Yes. And right now, I've trapped Medusa in a pit near the summit beneath a thick wall of ice. If you want to save the vampires and restore Harmony, then you'll need to go there and take her head."

CHAPTER TWENTY-TWO

The Garden of the Hesperides

The small, golden-winged Iris led Gertie through the rainbow arch over the Atlas Mountains. "Can you see him?"

Gertie narrowed her eyes and scanned the mountaintops for the giant Atlas. "In some versions, Heracles set him free."

"That's never going to happen."

Gertie felt sorry for the giant. He was condemned by Zeus to hold up the heavens, so they never reached the earth. This prevented Gaia and Uranus (Father Sky) from producing more Titans. More Titans would mean a threat to the established order.

"He's not usually visible to the human eye, but some demigods can see him, and since you're also a vampire…"

"I don't see him." Gertie clutched the hilt of the sword her grandmother had given her the day before, after she had fully recovered from the paralyzing effects of Zeus's thunderbolt. The sword and its scabbard had been crafted by Hephaestus.

"Then you may not be able to see his daughters, either, unless they show themselves to you."

Gertie knew that Atlas's daughters, known as the Hesperides, were three nymphs who guarded Hera's golden apple tree—a wedding gift from Gaia. The golden apples gave any who ate from them immortality. The Hesperides, along with a one-hundred headed serpent called Ladon, made sure that the apples didn't end up in the wrong hands.

"What about Ladon?" Gertie asked.

"Oh, you'll see *him*, all right." The goddess shuddered. "All those heads draping from the branches...a terrifying sight, indeed."

Gertie gripped the hilt with a sweaty hand and hoped she wouldn't have to use the sword. If only there was a more peaceful way to bring all of this to an end.

Just then, she got an idea. "Why doesn't Gaia threaten to take back the apple tree? Wouldn't Hera give you up to keep her tree?"

Iris turned and fluttered up to Gertie's eye level. "Once a god gives another god a gift, it can't be taken back. Poor form, that is."

The goddess turned and continued to lead the way to the base of the Atlas Mountains.

As they made their descent along the rainbow arch, Helios, the sun Titan, also made his descent toward the west. Soon, there would be no daylight left on this part of the world, and that meant the war with the vampires—presuming there were any remaining rebels not turned to stone—would continue in Athens. Gertie didn't even know if there were any vampires left fighting in the war. She hadn't spoken to Hector in three days and only knew that he and Jeno and Lajos were hunting Medusa. She'd tried to reach out to them telepathically but hadn't been able to make contact.

A part of her worried that they'd been killed, and her grandmother was lying to her. Maybe Gaia only cared about freeing Iris.

Her concern for her friends wasn't the only thing weighing on her mind. Gertie wondered how Hera would react to her proposition. Gaia had warned Gertie to be careful and had sent Iris as a guardian. Even though the Olympian queen helped Gertie fight against Dionysus and Poseidon for the eye of the Cyclops, there was no guarantee that the queen wouldn't try to kill her.

"Do you really think Hera will be willing to give you up if I can do this?" Gertie asked the winged goddess flittering beside her.

"I don't know," Iris replied. "But it's worth asking. The earth is in trouble."

When they stepped from the rainbow arch out onto the garden, Gertie braced herself for the possibility that the wine Gaia had given her to drink had worn off and the sunlight would burn. Luckily, she felt no pain. With that fear gone, she now stared at the huge, gnarly tree, with its sparkling, golden fruit, searching the branches for the hundred heads of Ladon. The green serpent's body was at first difficult to discern among the green foliage, but she was soon able to spot one pair of eyes, and then another, and another, and another...

A shiver snaked down Gertie's back. All one hundred heads lifted, and all two hundred eyes glared at her.

What had at first seemed like a tangled mess of thick roots at the base of the tree transformed into three dark-skinned goddesses with long brown hair. They wore long brown flowing robes and blended in with the trunk and roots of the tree until they moved forward.

"That's close enough," the one in the middle said.

Iris fluttered to the ground beside Gertie. "Hera is expecting us."

Just then, something swept down from the branches. Instinctively, Gertie drew her sword and stepped back. The thing coming at her, however, was not one of Ladon's hundred heads. It was a royal blue peacock, almost as large as the tree. Its beautiful feathers fanned out in glorious colors of blue, purple, and turquoise and were topped with more eyes staring down at Gertie as the bird landed before her.

"Put that sword away, unless you want me to leave," the peacock said.

"Hera?" Gertie sheathed the sword. "I was expecting an ox."

"I take both forms. Now tell me why we're here."

Gertie glanced down at Iris, who gave her a reassuring nod.

"I've come to make a deal," Gertie said.

"I'm listening."

"I want to help you take the vampires away from Dionysus." Gertie bit her lip.

"Go on."

"If I'm successful, I want you to release Iris from her servitude."

Hera squawked and made Gertie jump nearly a foot off the ground.

"Why in the world would I ever agree to such a thing?" the peacock shrieked. "I need her. Why should I give her up?"

Iris turned a shade of pink.

"I thought maybe your hate for Dionysus might be greater than your need for Iris," Gertie said.

"If I felt you had a chance of dethroning him as the lord of the vampires, then I might consider it." The peacock stretched its neck to look more closely into Gertie's eye. "Why do you want Iris?"

"I don't want her for myself," Gertie said. "The earth has been out of balance since you took her from Gaia."

"I see." The peacock turned as if she might fly away, but she turned back again. She was pacing. "Gaia sent you."

Gertie felt a cold sweat dripping down the back of her neck. Maybe this was a mistake.

"Just out of curiosity, how were you planning to dethrone Dionysus?" Hera asked.

"By taking Medusa's head and forcing Athena and the others to negotiate."

The peacock squawked again, but this time, it sounded more like laughter. "Oh, my."

The little bit of blood running through Gertie's veins rushed to her face and burned with anger. "What's so funny?"

"You do realize we gods actually hear your prayers, don't you?" Hera scoffed. "For many months, you have prayed to me to protect victims from being further victimized, citing Medusa as your greatest example. Do you really expect me to believe you're capable of taking her head? You won't do it. I can promise you that."

"Medusa had a chance at redemption," Gertie said through a tight throat. "She's not interested."

Hera laughed again. "You are quite entertaining, young demigod. I'll give you that. And you've got gumption."

"It's not gumption," Gertie said. "I have no choice."

Hera cocked her head to one side. "Gaia is *forcing* you?"

"No." Though Gertie wasn't sure how much she'd been manipulated. "It's the only way I can save the vampires from Athena. I wish I didn't have to kill Medusa, but I do."

"So, you're going through with this plan whether I make a deal with you or not?" Hera asked.

Gertie's face turned red again. She'd shown her entire hand to the *queen* of manipulation.

The peacock stretched its neck to peer into Gertie's eye once more. "What makes you think you can find Medusa before anyone else does?"

"I already know where she is."

"Where?"

"I won't tell you, unless you agree."

"You're bluffing."

"Am I?"

"Gaia has told her where Medusa is," Iris intervened. "The girl speaks the truth."

The peacock glared at Iris. "You *want* me to make this deal, don't you?"

"Everyone wants to be free, my queen. Please don't take it personally."

The peacock squawked again. "It makes no difference whether I parley with you, young demigod. You will never take Medusa's head. You don't have it in you."

"If that's true, then you have nothing to lose," Gertie said. "What harm would there be in you swearing on the river Styx to liberate Iris if I succeed, since you're so sure I won't?"

"None at all, I suppose," Hera admitted. "And to tell you the truth, I would gladly hand over my servant to see Dionysus dethroned. I really would."

"Then swear," Gertie said. "Swear on the river Styx that you'll set Iris free if I succeed."

The peacock stepped back and flapped its wings. "I swear." Then she lifted off the ground and disappeared in the clouds.

When Gertie lowered her gaze back to the tree, she noticed the three Hesperides were standing much closer to her than before, and the heads of the serpent—not all hundred, but enough—were closing in on her.

"Let's get out of here," Iris whispered.

Gertie turned on her heels and followed the winged goddess back to the rainbow as fast as she could run.

CHAPTER TWENTY-THREE

Preparations

Back in the cave with Gaia, Gertie listened closely as her grandmother showed her how to use the three-way-mirror shield. Gaia had recovered it from the stone body of a demigod who'd used it in his efforts to defeat Medusa way before the time of Perseus. Fashioned by Hephaestus, the ancient mirror-shield consisted of three round pieces that folded and unfolded like a cardboard display board. The shield was made almost entirely of titanium, including the hinges that connected the three parts, so it wasn't heavy. A handle protruded from the center piece, and the two side pieces folded back and could be clasped together as a single, thick, shield. To use the three-way mirror, you unclasped the side pieces and folded them toward the center handle until you were standing inside them. The pieces clicked into place, to keep them from flapping. By looking into them, you could see behind you in all directions, and you were protected on three sides.

The shield was as beautiful as it was useful. Each round piece was trimmed in a rope of gold, as was the handle in the center. The clasps were also made of gold.

"If at any time, you change your mind, just get out of there as quickly as you can," Gaia said. "But remember this: since you're a vampire, the only way she can destroy you—as long as you don't look at her—is by piercing your heart or by decapitation."

It suddenly occurred to Gertie that maybe her grandmother had wanted her to become a vampire all along, because it would increase

Gertie's chances of fulfilling the prophecy. Was it possible that Gaia had brought her and Jeno together?

Gertie tried not to think of it. She didn't want to believe that her grandmother had been using her. Instead, she recalled their sweet moments together when she was a little girl and held tightly to those memories.

Besides, Gertie was doing this to save the vampires, first and foremost. She *had* to save them, to save Jeno and herself. Although Hades had said he would help them, she no longer trusted her fate to any of the gods.

She did wish she could see Hector and Jeno and the others once more before facing Medusa—just in case she didn't make it out alive. She also wished she could see Mamá and Babá and her mother and father—Diane and James.

"Grandma, would you do me a favor, regardless of the outcome?" Gertie asked.

"What is it, dear?"

"Could you help Diane and James get back together? I really don't want them to get a divorce."

Gaia frowned. "Why is that important to you?"

Why *was* it important to Gertie? Up until recently, she'd resented the pair for their neglect. Yet, she supposed she'd always longed for their love and affection, and once she'd understood why they didn't give it to her, the love that had always been dormant inside her had overwhelmed her. "It would make me happy to know that they were happy. Please?"

She could tell by the look on her grandmother's face that Gertie's request didn't please her, but Gaia nodded and said, "Consider it done."

"Oh, thank you!" Gertie laid down the shield and hugged the goddess.

Gaia held her close and kissed her cheek. "You are my sweet, sweet child, Gertrude. You have been the light of my life for seventeen years. I want you to be happy."

Gertie squeezed her grandma's waist one more time before pulling away and taking back up the shield. "And while I'm asking for favors…"

Gaia arched a brow. "Yes?"

"If I don't make it out of your kneecap alive…"

"I won't let that happen to you," Gaia interrupted. "I will drop an avalanche on top of the monster if it looks like you're in trouble."

Gertie tried not to let her doubts show on her face, but she couldn't help but wonder if Gaia would really intervene if it meant the prophecy would not be fulfilled. She hoped so, and yet she supposed restoring Harmony to the earth had to take priority over one grandchild, so maybe she couldn't fault her grandmother for taking such a risk with Gertie's life. "Just in case something goes wrong…"

"Yes?"

"Could you please tell Hector, and Jeno, and my other friends that I…" Gertie fought tears. The thought of never seeing them again suddenly made her throat catch. "That I said goodbye and I love them?"

"That won't be necessary." Gaia stroked her hair.

"But if it is…"

"Of course."

"One other thing," Gertie said.

"Yes?"

"If I have any chance of defeating Medusa, I need to feed."

Gaia lifted a finger in the air. "I know just the place to send you."

"*Send* me? You mean you can't take me there?" Gertie's chest got tight.

"I'm afraid that when the Olympians took over, my chariot was confiscated, and god travel wouldn't be safe right now. It would be best if you traveled on foot. You'll want to avoid the sea and sky."

Gertie shook her head in disbelief. Gaia's kneecap was Mount Everest, which was all the way in China. This was the first that Gertie had heard that she'd have to get herself there on her own. She felt a sweat coming on, and it was a cold one.

"How will I find my way? I've never even been to China."

"Right now, we're below Turkey, which is just across the sea from Greece. We're near the southern border, not far from Cyprus. Can you picture where we are on the map?"

Gertie nodded. Her knowledge of world geography had really sucked before she'd left New York to come to Athens, but ever since the uprising, she'd paid attention.

"From here, it's a straight shot across Iran, Afghanistan, Pakistan, and India."

"I have to cross the Middle East? Where all the wars are going on?" Gertie bit down so hard on her lip, that she made it bleed.

"Ares does make a lot of mischief there," Gaia agreed.

"Just great."

"It'll be nighttime," Gaia assured her. "They rarely fight at night."

"At least, we hope," Gertie muttered.

"Mount Everest sits between Nepal and Tibet. Be sure to cross India to the north of the Himalayas, so that you enter Tibet. And just up the mountain is a Buddhist monastery. There are at least twenty monks and ten nuns living there. That's where I want you to feed. It's isolated. It will be dark. And they'll be sleeping. If they wake, maybe they'll think they're having a spiritual experience. It's the perfect plan."

It didn't sound like the perfect plan to Gertie. "Why can't we travel there from down here, in the Underworld?"

"Hades will sense us, he'll take over, and you'll have no bargaining tool. Hera swore to free Iris if *you* succeed. If Hades takes Medusa's head, the prophecy has no chance of being fulfilled."

"But how will I find my way? How will I know how to get there?" Gertie's heart raced. She hadn't realized she'd be traveling so far on her own. She'd always had Jeno or Hector with her. Facing Medusa was scary enough without having to cross the world on foot alone.

"I'll give you a compass. Stay due east—except you'll have to go around the Caspian Sea. If you keep going east in a straight line, you'll eventually see the Himalayas. Once you cross into Tibet and see Mount Everest, head south. If you run at your top speed, you should get there in less than eight hours. You'll find the pit with Medusa by looking for the blood-red ice I used to trap her." Gaia put her hands on Gertie's shoulders. "I know you can do this. You have the speed and the vision of a vampire. And you have a heart of gold. If anyone can do this, you can."

Gertie gave her a weak nod.

"Just try your best to go as fast as you can," Gaia added. "The longer this takes, the more hardened those who have been turned to stone become. If we wait too long…"

"How much time do they have?" Gertie asked.

"No one really knows, but I've not seen anyone recovered with the eye of Polyphemus who'd been turned for more than a week."

Gertie counted the days on her fingers since Medusa had appeared in Athens. Six days.

"Now put on this breast plate. It will protect you from both the front and the back, if Medusa attempts to pierce your heart."

The breast plate was light, like the shield, and also made of titanium, but it didn't have the gold rope trim. There was gold on the front, in the image of a golden apple tree. The artwork was quite beautiful.

Gaia helped Gertie put it on. Leather straps secured it at the shoulders and at the sides just above her waist. It wasn't too big or bulky. In fact, it felt as though it had been made for her.

Over the next few minutes, she felt like she was in a daze as Gaia strapped items to Gertie's belt: a compass, a canteen of wine, a knife, and the scabbard and sword. The shield fit across her back, like another piece of armor, and was held there by a leather sash that fed through the handle—which faced out so that the shield was flat against the back of the breastplate, the top of it reaching the center of the back of her head. One tug on the end of the sash would free the shield in an instant.

"Ready?" Gaia asked.

Gertie gave her another weak nod. She wasn't ready, but she had no choice.

Gaia led her from the cave through an ascending tunnel where the fire of the Phlegethon River did not flow. Luckily, Gertie's vampire vision was as sharp in pure darkness as it was in the light of day. In fact, Gertie had come to realize that her vision was best in pitch darkness.

The eyes of a vampire were made for darkness, she remembered Jeno saying once.

Oh, Jeno, I hope you're alive.

Gertie? Where are you? Jeno's voice sounded in her head.

Gertie froze in her tracks. *Jeno? Is that really you?*

"Everything okay?" Gaia asked from up ahead.

"Yes." She was afraid to admit that she thought she'd heard Jeno. *Jeno?*

As she continued the ascent along the winding tunnel behind Gaia, she heard no more from him, but she didn't stop trying to reach him. Over and over, in her mind, she called out his name.

The tunnel spiraled up and up, and they soon reached a large opening that led to the upperworld.

"This leads to the outskirts of the city of Adana. Follow your compass due east. If you get lost, just pray to me, and I will help you find your way. Always remember that I am just beneath your feet."

Gaia kissed Gertie, who said nothing as she took a deep breath and climbed out into the open air.

CHAPTER TWENTY-FOUR

To Gaia's Kneecap, or Mount Everest

Night was just beginning to fall over the southern shoreline of Turkey as Gertie ran at her full speed due east. She imagined Hector running in front of her so she wouldn't feel alone. She pretended to stare at his back.

She spoke to him and to Jeno as she ran, hoping to hear one of their voices in her head again. She'd begun to suspect that maybe she hadn't heard Jeno after all. Maybe it had been her imagination.

After a while, something ironic occurred to Gertie. All her life she'd been an avid reader of adventure stories, and here she was in the middle of one. It was almost as if she'd leapt into the pages of one of her books. She pinched herself and blinked many times, hoping that she would wake up and find it had all been a dream.

No, she was glad this was real. The life she'd been leading before going to Athens hadn't been much of a life at all. She'd been emotionally estranged from her parents and had made no friends. Now she had multiple parents—not all who loved her, but many who did. And she had multiple friends—more than you could count on one hand, even. She had Hector and Jeno and Nikita and Klaus and Phoebe and Lajos. Tears sprang to her eyes, and she was filled with gratitude. No matter what her future held, she was glad she was living this present.

And getting to know Jeno and Hector—even if she never saw either of them again—had fulfilled her in ways nothing else could. Parental love and approval could only get a person so far. Jeno and Hector were both amazing people whom she deeply loved, and they had deeply loved her back. Some people didn't get that in their lifetime, and she'd gotten it twice. Even though she was about to face a fierce and dangerous monster, she felt like the luckiest girl in the world, now that she thought about it. Now that she thought about it, she had become a powerful badass with the chance to save an entire race of people while restoring balance to the earth. Now that she thought about it, she totally rocked.

Her foot caught on a root and she fell in the mud.

She got up and brushed off the mud, glancing around. Had something or someone caused her to trip?

She checked her compass and took off running again, with slightly less confidence.

Soon she was running along the side of a river. It wasn't long, however, when that river met another. Should she go around it? If so, how far north would she have to run? Gertie slowed to a stop, full of indecision, wishing Gaia had given her better directions. Stay east was all she had said. This river wasn't too wide, so she took a chance and flew over it, landing safely on the other side.

Thank goodness.

She checked her compass again and continued on her way.

Another thought occurred to her. As a reader, she'd come to recognize certain patterns in the adventure stories she consumed, and one such pattern was that if the hero of the story felt like all was lost before the great climax, the story would almost always end in a victory; however, if the hero had a revelation before the climax, feeling gratitude and contentment with the life he or she'd been given no matter the outcome, the story ended in tragedy.

Gertie swallowed hard and reminded herself that this wasn't an adventure story. Just because she had felt contentment, that didn't mean she was going to die.

About two hours had passed when she finally reached the Caspian Sea. She followed the shoreline south until she was running to the east again. From here, her vampire eyes could make out the Himalaya Mountains in the distance, with Mount Everest the tallest among them. This filled her with renewed confidence. As long as she could see the mountains, she knew she was heading in the right direction.

She could tell she was near a heavily populated city, because the sweet smell of human blood permeated the air. Her mouth watered. It had been days since she'd last fed, and she was starving.

Even after she'd passed the sea, the sweet smell of human blood was all around her. She ran into a group of mountains, not as massive as the Himalayas, and nestled in a quiet valley full of snow was a small village. Gertie slowed down and wondered if she should feed. Gaia wanted her to wait until she reached the monastery, but it was still hours away.

As she walked through the village, she used her x-ray vision to scan the interiors for people. In one of the houses, an old man was still awake and reading by candlelight. In most of the houses she passed, she could also see at least one dog or cat, and she'd learned in her short life as a vampire to avoid them. They alarmed the humans. The only way to quiet them was with a bite, and since their blood tasted terrible, it wasn't worth it. She was about to give up when she came to a tiny house on the edge of the village. Through the walls, she saw four sleeping humans and no pets. She made her way to the room where the two children slept.

With all her armor and weapons, it was difficult to be quiet, and by the time she reached the bedroom, one of the children was sitting up in her bed with her eyes wide open.

Gertie almost turned around and left, but her hunger compelled her forward.

The little girl pulled her blanket over her head. This was enough to make Gertie go for the other child, the one still asleep. Quickly, she dug her fangs into the boy's tender neck and sucked the sweet blood down. Her body rejoiced, and she felt so heavenly, that, for a moment, she was tempted to drain the boy, but she came to her senses and stopped at just over a pint.

The boy opened his eyes and looked up at her, momentarily dazed and paralyzed by the virus. Before he had a chance to open his mouth and speak, she commanded him to close his eyes and go back to sleep. The boy, thankfully, obeyed.

The girl, however, had peeked from beneath her blanket and stared in shock at Gertie and her brother. Gertie glared at her, attempting to use mind control to get her to fall asleep like her brother. But Gertie could tell the girl was resisting, and in another horrible moment, she realized the child had opened her mouth and had uttered a shrill cry.

Gertie jumped from the bed and flew from the house but was attacked by a barrage of bullets before making her escape. Panting and full of panic, she flew all the way around a mountain before she stopped to assess her wounds: two gunshots to the back of her calf.

And the delicious blood she'd gone to all that trouble to drink was pouring from them.

She sat on the side of the mountain, quickly scooping handfuls of ice and snow onto her leg and after many minutes was able to stop the last of the precious blood from leaking out.

She closed her eyes and cried in frustration. If anybody had been there to see her, she might have fought the tears, but, since she was alone, she let them fall. She wasn't even halfway to Mount Everest and she'd already wasted valuable time.

Stick to the plan, Gertie, she said to herself.

Once her wounds had healed, she climbed to her feet, checked her compass, and headed east, around the mountain, running as fast as she could. She wouldn't be able to make up the lost time, but she wouldn't waste another minute. If the vampires that had been turned to stone weren't restored soon, they could be lost forever.

Although she was tempted to save time and fly across the river bordering Iran and Afghanistan, she worried Zeus or one of the wind gods would see her and ruin everything, so she took to the city and crossed a bridge by foot. There were few cars on the road this late at night, and as soon as she could get away from the city, she did. She had to cross another rugged mountain range before she reached Kabul, and when she did, she felt happy, because she knew she was almost there.

Oh, Jeno. I wish you were here to keep me on track. You're always so good at keeping time.

Gertie? Where are you? Jeno's voice entered her head.

Gertie slowed her pace but didn't stop running. *Jeno? Can you hear me?*

Oh my gods, yes! Where are you? I've been looking everywhere for you!

I can't tell you. I promised Gaia.

I beg you to tell me. I've been worried out of my mind. So has Hector.

Hector? Is he with you?

Yes. We're on the island of Crete. Lajos is here as well. When you went missing, we were told you might be hidden in the labyrinth.

No.

Then where are you?

At that moment, as Gertie crossed a bridge over a river and into a canyon, the ground began to shake, and an avalanche quaked down a mountainside about two hundred yards from where Gertie was running. Right away, she knew what was happening. Gaia was interfering with Gertie's ability to communicate with Jeno.

"Please, Gaia! I won't tell him! Just let me talk to him!"

Gertie kept running and calling out to Jeno, but she heard nothing. She was half-tempted to stop and give up her quest, just to get back at her grandmother. If the lives of the vampires weren't at stake, she'd seriously consider it. But she kept running toward Mount Everest because she had no choice.

The next two hours went by fast. Gertie was distracted with figuring out how to safely cross rivers without being spotted by Poseidon or Zeus or any of their deities. Sometimes she managed to find a bridge, and sometimes she took a chance and flew or swam. At one point, she happened upon a group of campers around a fire. They were awake and sharing stories. She'd been so focused that she hadn't even sensed them until she was practically on top of them. When they spotted her, they looked up at her in horror. One of them called her a demon. As another fetched his rifle, she took to the air.

When she finally reached Tibet and could see Mount Everest looming before her to the south, she smiled with relief. Her fangs protruded of their own accord, because this also meant that she was only an hour away from feasting on monks, and she was hungry.

CHAPTER TWENTY-FIVE

Medusa

Revitalized from the blood of twenty monks, Gertie continued her ascent up Mount Everest. Dawn broke in the Far East, and Helios began his journey across the sky in his golden cup. Gertie took a swig of wine from her canteen to stop the prickling sensation on her skin. Then she returned the cap and continued toward the summit.

For the first time since beginning this journey, she began to think about facing Medusa. Before now, she'd been too distracted with finding her way. Now that she'd made it this far, the ramifications of what she was about to attempt boiled within her.

Medusa had been a young, beautiful, and innocent nymph. Poseidon seduced—some say raped—her in Athena's temple. When Athena caught them in the act, instead of going after Poseidon, Athena punished the victim. Athena made her into a monster with snakes for hair and eyes that turned all onlookers into cold, hard stone, making it impossible for Medusa to ever have a friend or a lover. The injustice of this played over and over in Gertie's mind.

And the destruction of this same victim was now necessary to save a race of other victims. But did the ends justify the means? Was it okay to kill Medusa to save the vampires?

"Medusa had her chance at redemption," Gertie mumbled to herself in the thin air. She was a third of the way up the mountain—half flying, half climbing, since the slope was so steep in places.

Maybe Hera had been right. Maybe Gertie didn't have what it took to go through with it.

"I have to do it," Gertie mumbled, trying to keep her hands steady. "I have no choice." A wave of heat crawled over her cold skin.

A streak of lightning flashed across the sky, followed by a crack of thunder. Had Gertie been spotted by Zeus? Maybe it was impossible to climb this high and not be seen by the lord of the sky. With greater vigilance than before, Gertie continued her way up the mountain, avoiding flight—though she found her knees and ankles shook with fear. She was afraid to kill Medusa, yet she was *more* afraid of being killed by her.

Another jolt of lightning cut across the sky, and this time, it hit the summit of Mount Everest, causing an avalanche down the southern slope. It rumbled angrily and shook the entire mountain. If the avalanche had come this way, down the northern side, Gertie would have had no choice but to fly and be completely exposed to Zeus. She crouched and clung to the rock as she scaled her way up, praying to Gaia to protect her.

When she finally reached the northern ridge, she was able to look down at the ice caps below and spot the one stained red. The colors of the sun cast golds and oranges on the ice, but the red stain was unmistakable. It marked Medusa's trap.

"This is it," Gertie whispered through a chattering jaw. "The moment of truth."

As cold as it was up this high in the ice and snow, Gertie's jaw didn't chatter because her body couldn't take the elements; Gertie's jaw chattered because she was utterly terrified.

She released her shield from its leather sash and, keeping it folded for now, gripped it tightly as she made her way down toward the red ice cap.

All it takes is one glimpse.

She wondered if Hades would use the eye of Polyphemus to save her if she was turned to stone. No, Medusa wouldn't allow that. If she turned Gertie to stone, Medusa would crush her into a hundred fragments, for sure.

Gertie edged down the smooth and slick side of the ridge, flying part way to keep from falling. When she neared the red ice cap, she unsheathed her sword and pierced the tip into the heart of the blood-red stain. The ice shattered beneath her feet. She held herself aloft and didn't dare look down into the pit without her shield.

The monster beneath her hissed.

Gertie sheathed her sword and unfolded the shield. As she hovered above the deep pit, trembling with fear, she sought Medusa. Another bolt of lightning struck the mountain, causing ice to crumble and fall all around her. Luckily, none of it reached the pit. Maybe Gaia had something to do with that.

Not wanting to get struck by Zeus again, Gertie jumped into Gaia's kneecap with the shield guarding her on three sides. She landed on her feet, unsheathed her sword, and turned around and around, gazing into the shield for the monster's reflection. The pit was at least a hundred feet deep and fifty feet in diameter.

"It's about time," Medusa growled. "I wondered how long I'd be trapped in here."

"I didn't come to rescue you."

"I suspected as much. I can never catch a break."

"Hades tried to give you one, but you turned it down."

Medusa didn't reply.

Gertie wondered if she'd been given false information. "You did turn it down, didn't you? Your chance at redemption?" She still hadn't spotted Medusa. She turned around and around, using the shield to peer into every nook and cranny of the deep crevasse. Gertie sensed her, but her head pulsed with terror, making it more difficult to discern her surroundings. Her heart raced, causing her to pant like a runner.

"You wouldn't understand," Medusa said in an accusing tone.

"Try me." At last, she spotted the monster, up high on a cliff edge, about twenty feet below the opening of the pit. Was she climbing her way out?

"Fine. You might not believe this, but, when I was young, I was *in love* with Poseidon," Medusa said. "Yet I respected his wife and kept my distance, admiring him from afar."

Gertie trained her eyes on Medusa's reflection in the three-way shield, ready for any sudden movement. The monster seemed to be inching her way up toward the mouth of the pit.

"I loved the sea and everything in it, including him. He was master of all I enjoyed, of all of my delights. I swam every day and sang songs to him. I once had a beautiful voice."

Gertie could make out tears forming in the stone-white sockets of Medusa's face as she scaled up another few inches toward the top.

"One day, I was racing with the dolphins, when a pelican pecked me on my head as I was leaping up from the sea. I ignored him at first, but when I leapt again, he pecked me a second time. Finally I stopped to complain. He interrupted me with a message. Amphitrite was looking for a servant to help her with Poseidon's castle. If I was interested, I was to meet her in Athens on the acropolis at dusk."

"So, you thought you were going to meet with Poseidon's wife?"

"Precisely."

"Then what happened?"

"Waiting for me outside of the Parthenon was a handsome white steed," Medusa said. "He asked me to climb on his back, and he'd deliver me to my new mistress. I did as he asked."

"And did he take you to Amphitrite?" Gertie asked.

"No." Medusa's voice became harsh again. "He took me into the Parthenon. He galloped around the temple, around and around, making me dizzy. Then at some point, he changed into Poseidon, and I found my legs wrapped around his hips. He held me at my waist and told me he loved me just before he kissed me."

Gertie gasped.

"It was the most amazing kiss of my life. The only kiss of my life. I was so enamored and swept off my feet that I barely understood what was happening. Then Athena walked in and found us."

"Is that when Athena had her revenge on you?" Gertie asked.

"Not at first. She glared at Poseidon, who went on to invent some lie about *me* tricking *him*. Without giving me a chance to explain or defend myself, Athena cast her curse on me."

Both Gertie and Medusa were silent for several seconds. Nearly a whole minute had gone by when Gertie said, "I'm so sorry."

"I can't believe a single god won't seek justice on my behalf," Medusa said. "Even after I screamed my defense at Athena, after she'd already made me a Gorgon, she continued to hate me. She hated me so much, she wanted my head on her shield like a hunter prizes the antlers from his kill."

"What about Hades? He's offered you redemption."

"That's not the same as justice."

No, it wasn't. "So what do you plan to do?"

"Get my own justice."

"How?"

"I'm going to ruin Poseidon."

Gertie tried to swallow but found all the moisture had left her mouth, and her throat was as dry as hot sand. She noticed Medusa had climbed within five feet of the opening of the pit. Soon Gertie would have to do something to stop her. "Are you sure that's a good idea?"

"He ruined *me*, did he not?"

"You still have time to turn things around and make a new life for yourself."

Medusa laughed.

"Why is that funny?"

"I could never be happy as long as Poseidon went unpunished. If the gods won't serve him justice, I will."

At that moment, Medusa climbed from the pit onto the side of the mountain.

Gertie flew up after her, using the shield to guide her, and landed about twenty feet away. "Poseidon's whole kingdom will suffer if you go after him, and you'll only create more victims. There's got to be another way."

"There isn't!" Medusa cried.

"Maybe we can ask for all the gods to come up with a suitable punishment. I've read that both Apollo and Ares have had to serve time as barn boys on earth."

Medusa laughed again. "That's not going to happen."

"No! But neither are your plans!" screeched the owl of Athena from overhead just before she revealed her true form.

"Athena!" Medusa shrieked.

The goddess landed on a ridge high above them. Gertie could see in the reflection of her shield Medusa panicking behind her—her snake hair writhing in fear. In that instant, Gertie knew she could not kill her to save the vampires. Instead, she would protect her.

"Wait!" Gertie screamed at Athena and backed up, moving closer to Medusa. "Please! I beg you to hear me out!"

"I'm listening, but not for long!" Athena shouted.

"The gods have done an injustice to Medusa," Gertie said. "There must be a way to make it right. Can't Poseidon be made to…"

Gertie glanced down at her shield only to be shocked by the sight of the monster about to attack her from behind. In a flurry of panic, Gertie fumbled for her sword. She was unable to unsheathe it fast enough. Medusa was nearly on her. Gertie grabbed the knife, and, with her eyes closed, she turned on the monster and plunged the knife into her heart.

Medusa screamed, and her snake hair hissed.

Thinking quickly, Gertie left the knife and, with eyes still closed, reached for the hissing hair. Then, with both hands, Gertie snapped Medusa's neck with all her strength, screaming with fear and determination as she twisted the head of the monster from its body. For five horrible seconds, the snakes writhed in her hands before falling still and silent. Then Gertie opened her eyes, without looking at the head, and turned to face Athena above her.

Gertie was trembling and crying, unlike any hero she had ever read about, but she didn't care. She glared at the goddess of war and wisdom and said, "I'll give you this, on one condition."

CHAPTER TWENTY-SIX

A Deal with Gods

A s Gertie gripped the head of Medusa, the ground beneath her feet trembled. Athena turned into an owl and flapped her wings in astonishment as Gertie shot up into the sky on a pillar of ice into the clear blue sky. It suddenly occurred to Gertie what was happening: Gaia was delivering her to Iris, who waited above in her rainbow arch.

Once Gertie was inside the rainbow beside the winged goddess, she fell to her knees and wept. Her heart pounded a million beats per second, even though it was finally over. She dared not let go of the head of Medusa, but she felt sick to her stomach that she'd had to kill her.

"Why did she attack me?" Gertie asked Iris. "I was trying to help her."

Iris said nothing and waited patiently for Gertie to dry her eyes with her one free, trembling, hand.

"Ready?" Iris asked.

Gertie climbed to her feet and nodded.

The winged goddess led her across the rainbow and into a cluster of clouds. Iris poured her golden pitcher of water into them, and they immediately thickened and became gray. Gertie wondered how such a tiny pitcher could fill up the massive clouds, but she shrugged and thought it must be magic.

"This way," Iris said.

Gertie followed her onto the cluster, and then in another instant, they were flying across the heavens toward Greece. As they flew, the rain poured onto the earth below until they were empty, at which time another rainbow appeared, stretching toward Mount Olympus.

"Come on," Iris said as she flew from the clouds to the arch.

Gertie followed, still clutching the head of Medusa.

At the gate to Olympus, Iris said, "Spring, Summer, Winter, and Fall, please open the gate so that I, Iris, goddess of the rainbow, and Gertrude, daughter to Dionysus and Philomena, may enter to address our leaders."

The clouds parted, and Gertie followed Iris past the whale fountain and up the steps into the palace of the gods.

Athena had beat them there, and she now stood on her throne in her natural form and glared down at them.

Hera stood, too, but she had a smile on her face—a smile of both surprise and glee.

Zeus did not stand but sat frowning. "Tell us your intentions," he commanded.

Gertie glanced around at the thrones that circled the perimeter of the court. All the gods were present except for Hades, Persephone, and Poseidon—and Dionysus, as usual. She couldn't proceed without them.

Demeter also wasn't there, since at this time of year, she lived in her winter cabin.

"I've come to offer Athena the head of Medusa, but with conditions," she said. "And I won't state them until Hades, Poseidon, and Dionysus are present, too."

Zeus turned to Hermes. "As fast as you can."

"Yes, my lord." Hermes disappeared.

"I didn't think you had it in you," Hera said.

"Nor I," Ares said beside his mother.

"Neither did I," Gertie admitted with an extreme blush crossing her face. "But Medusa gave me no choice. Even when I tried to help her, she came at me."

"Well done!" Aphrodite cheered.

Gertie turned and gave her a smile.

"Yes, well done," Hephaestus said. "Hector will be proud and relieved."

Gertie turned to the god of the forge. "Do you know where he is?"

"On a ferry from Crete to Patras."

"Are Jeno and Lajos with him?"

"I believe so," Hephaestus said.

"Yes," Apollo confirmed. "And I see you reunited with them soon."

Gertie took a deep breath and held back her tears of relief. She couldn't wait to see them.

She was surprised when Artemis, the goddess of the hunt and Apollo's twin sister, left her throne and approached her. "You, my dear, are one badass. Don't you ever forget it." The goddess didn't wait for Gertie to reply. She turned on her heel and stepped back onto her throne.

Gertie gawked at the goddess, totally shocked by this sign of approval. Artemis continued to smile upon Gertie with a twinkle in her eye. Gertie beamed with pride.

A sound at the palace entrance attracted the attention of all present. Gertie pivoted in time to see Poseidon cross the room to his throne. He scowled at her, though she wondered why, when she'd just saved him and his kingdom from a threat.

In the next instant, Hermes appeared at his throne with Dionysus beside him.

"And Lord Hades?" Zeus asked.

"Here," the lord of the Underworld called from the entrance as he crossed into the court. A throne emerged from the floor of the palace in front of the entrance, completing the circle of deities. Whether it came all the way up from the Underworld, Gertie did not know. Hades took his seat and waited patiently for her to begin.

"What are these conditions?" Athena demanded.

Gertie turned to face the goddess of war and wisdom. "I want you to swear on the river Styx that you'll never harm the remaining vampires of Athens. They are your people, too, and you should love and protect them as much as the others."

Athena narrowed her eyes at Gertie. "The vampires are responsible for the degradation of my city—poverty and addiction. Their very existence requires them to manipulate and deceive and make dependent their victims. Moreover, it is selfish of vampires to live beyond their natural years on the blood of others. They have had their lives. They need to move on and allow others to live theirs."

"They can't help what the gods made them to be," Gertie said. "And Hades has a plan for them. I will give you the head of Medusa, Athena, if you and the other gods will agree to acknowledge Hades as the new leader of the vampires. It's too late for Medusa. She cared only about seeking vengeance on Poseidon. But, except for a few who've already been destroyed, the vampires of Athens are innocent."

"You wish to dethrone your own father?" Dionysus interrupted.

"When were you ever a father to me?" Gertie said as tears suddenly flooded her eyes.

"Did I not save your life more than once from the threat of the vampires?" he asked.

"You only helped me when it suited you. There were plenty of other times I needed you, and you weren't there. You even took the helm of invisibility from me when I was trying to end the war peacefully."

"Because you had taken the side of Hades," Dionysus accused.

"The noble side," she said. "What have you ever done for the vampires? Every so often over the centuries, you'd mention the possibility of an uprising, but you never did anything. *I* did something. *I* brought about the uprising. *My friends and I* did everything, and you never lifted a finger to help us."

Hades stood from his throne. "If the council will agree to make me the lord of the vampires, I will use the eye of Polyphemus to lift Medusa's curse on them. Then I will instill them with purpose as they help Thanatos collect the souls of the dead. They can feed on fresh human carcasses and no longer be a threat to human life."

Athena lifted a palm in the air, like a witness being sworn into court. "I'll agree so long as no more vampires are made. If another one is turned, the maker's head will join Medusa's on my shield."

"Hear, hear!" Artemis cried.

Gertie's stomach formed a knot. No more vampires meant she wouldn't be able to turn Hector. Should she try to negotiate for that exception? Or would that endanger her chances of making her deal?

"Are all in agreement then?" Zeus asked.

"Not all," Dionysus said.

"You don't count." Hera smiled cruelly at him. "You've never counted."

"Wait!" Gertie cried. "One more thing!"

Athena rolled her eyes at Gertie. "What now?"

"I will give you this head if you turn the vampires over to Hades *and* if you support Dionysus's right to be a part of this court."

"Deal," Athena said.

Hera's face turned the color of a tomato. "You double crosser!"

"I kept my word," Gertie said. "And even though I have issues with my father, he *does* count."

Gertie glanced at Dionysus, who seemed stunned into silence. Maybe no one had ever stood up for him before. Zeus looked pleased as punch as he climbed to his feet, calmed his wife, and said, "Do all swear on the river Styx to agree to these terms?"

All but Hera agreed.

CHAPTER TWENTY-SEVEN

Back to New York

Gertie sat between the wings of the giant white crane as they flew across the night sky from Mount Olympus to Patras. She could have flown herself, but the god of the forge offered, and who was she to refuse him?

He delivered her directly to the port to await the ferry from Crete. The others standing around on the docks could not see the beautiful crane deliver the girl to stand among them, but when she shifted from invisibility mode by releasing the energy she'd been holding in, she startled a few of the people beside her. She smiled and waved, as the white crane, still invisible to the others, flew away. The people beside her probably thought she was a little off. At least she wasn't still wearing the breastplate and weapons. Instead, she wore a glamour consisting of jeans and a hoodie.

Jeno was the first to step off the boat. When he met her eyes, they lit up, and a smile cracked his face in half. Hector and Lajos were right behind him. When Hector's eyes met hers, she was surprised to see them flood with tears. He'd never cried in front of her before, and here he was, on the brink of crying like a baby.

He ran to her, and her heart rejoiced.

He circled his arms around her waist and buried his face in her shoulder as he let his tears flow.

She wrapped her arms around his neck and caressed his hair, trying to comfort him. A check of his mind revealed that he had never been as afraid in his entire life as he'd been the past few days.

"I was scared I'd never find you again," he said. "After Apollo gave you the elixir, you went missing."

"Gaia took me," she said.

"Jeno told me," Hector said. "She's the one who told us you were in the labyrinth."

"She was afraid you'd interfere with my role in a prophecy. I'll tell you all about it later."

Hector hugged her again and said, "I'm so freaking proud of you."

"We all are," Lajos said beside them.

She smiled first at Lajos, and then at Jeno. His mind was blocked, but she could read his face. He wanted his hug, too.

After kissing Hector's cheek, she released him and embraced Jeno. He didn't hold her as long or as tightly as Hector had. He whispered, "I'm so glad you're safe." Then he let her go.

Lajos hugged her last.

"Will you be staying here with your aunt now?" she asked him.

"Eventually," he said. "But tonight, I want to fly back with you and the guys."

"Fly back where?" she asked him.

"New York," Jeno said.

Hector tugged the ends of her hair. "Everyone's waiting to see you."

"And I don't want to miss the reunion," Lajos said.

Hector grinned. "I think he just wants to see Nikita."

They all four laughed.

She tried to read Jeno's mind again. The guard against her was strong. "And how are we flying? By plane?"

"No way," Jeno said with a smile. "We're going the old-fashioned way, like old times."

They all laughed again.

"Okay then," she said. "I'm ready when you are."

Lajos convinced Jeno to bite him so he could fly on his own for once. Since Jeno hadn't fed in quite some time, it didn't take much to get him to agree.

Jeno flew on one side of Gertie and Lajos on the other, while she carried Hector across the dark sky over first Europe and then the Atlantic. As they flew, Lajos turned somersaults along the way and pretty much entertained himself as Jeno told her everything he'd learned from his cousins who had lived in the caves of Crete. While on the ferry, Jeno had been told by his cousins telepathically that Hades had already lifted Medusa's curse and had made the announcement to those in the Underworld about following him. Hades had also been to Athens, to Crete, and to other parts of Greece in his chariot to rescue any he hadn't already taken to his realm. Vampires from neighboring cities—both those who had and who had not participated in the uprising—heard of Hades's call and gleefully accepted the opportunity to instill purpose in their hard lives. A few vampires chose to ignore the call and would continue to live as paupers in the shadows of humans, but Jeno thought more and more of them would flock to Hades once they saw what a good life the others had there.

Then Hector asked her to tell them all about her battle with Medusa. She told them about the three-way shield and her journey across the Middle East to Mount Everest. She mentioned her mistake at the village and getting shot and her feast at the Tibetan monastery. She described the ascent up Mount Everest and the blood-stained ice cap and how she used her sword to shatter the ice. She told them all about the deep pit and Medusa's story of what happened with Poseidon. Then she told them how she had stood up to Athena for Medusa, only to barely escape with her life when Medusa attacked her from behind.

Her story was interrupted by the appearance of three women flying toward them. Although they looked younger and more beautiful than the last time she'd seen them, Gertie recognized the three vampires as the women who had once accosted her near Omonoia Square.

"You," the one in the middle said in Greek as they flew past.

Gertie glanced behind her in time to see one on the end wave and say, "Thank you."

"Are they already collecting souls?" Gertie asked her friends.

"Oh, yes," Jeno said. "Hades is very organized."

The four laughed again.

"Now tell us what happened on Mount Olympus," Hector insisted.

It felt amazing to hold him in her arms. His mind was full of affection for her, and of longing, and of pride. He held onto her waist and gazed into her eyes, occasionally resting his chin on her head as she relayed the deal she'd made with the gods and how she'd made it.

"I'm sure Dionysus will be happier with a vote on Mount Olympus than he ever was as lord of the vampires," Jeno said when she'd finished her story.

When they finally reached Staten Island, dusk had just come to this side of the world. They entered Gertie's house to find everyone gathered in the living room, including James, Gertie's father. Gaia must have kept her promise.

Diane and Mamá and Babá were on their feet with open arms to greet her. After she'd hugged each of them, she grabbed Nikita and held her tight.

"I was so scared I'd lost you," Gertie said through tears.

"*You* were scared?" Nikita said. "Man, oh, man. I'm just so glad to see you."

Next was Klaus. Even though she'd been told by Gaia that he was back from the dead, seeing him with her own eyes filled her with relief. "Thank the gods," she said as she hugged him.

"No, thank *you*," he said. "I'm alive because of *you*."

Phoebe came around and hugged her next. "Thank you, Gertie," she said. "Thank you for all you've done for me and for my family."

Gertie was overcome with tears. She hugged Phoebe hard and kissed the top of her head.

James was the last to be embraced. She couldn't actually remember ever hugging him. That was so sad to her now. She wondered if it was sad to him, too. She reached into his mind to find fear and confusion.

"Your mom told me everything," he said to her. "I'm still trying to wrap my head around it all."

She looked up at him and nodded. "I get it. It's a lot to take in."

"Maybe we can start over?" he asked.

She gave him a smile and a nod. "Sure."

He held out his arms, and though she was afraid, and it felt really awkward, she went to him. He kissed the top of her head. Unexpectedly, she broke down into more tears. She wasn't sure why or how to explain it, so she didn't try. James patted her on the back and kissed her hair again before she awkwardly pulled away. Hector was there at her side. He took her hand and gave it a reassuring squeeze.

"We have some good news," Babá announced. "Oh, can we tell them yet?" He looked first at James and then at Diane.

"Why not?" Diane said.

"Tell us what?" Nikita asked. "What's going on?" She let go of Lajos's hand and went up to her father. "Tell us what?"

Babá looked across the room at James, who gave him a nod. "The Morgans are coming to live with us in Athens."

Gertie's mouth dropped open. "What?" She went to her mother. "Is this true? We're moving to Athens?"

"I've decided I want my company to help rebuild what was once a great city," James said.

Diane put an arm around her husband's waist. "The news stations have been reporting on the devastation over there."

"I know my people can help," James said. "Starting with the American school. I've already sent a team of engineers over there. Classes should open again next month."

"So all of you can go back to school!" Mamá cried happily.

Gertie blushed. "Well, not me."

"Yes, you can," Hector said. "A sip of wine each morning, and you can tolerate the sun."

"And then at night, you can help me in the Underworld," Jeno said.

Gertie put her hands to her cheeks, her face ablaze with surprise and wonder. Too many emotions were churning through her. "It sounds like you all have it figured out."

"But we lost everything in the fire," Klaus said. "Where are we going to live? And the restaurant where you worked, Babá? Is it still there? Do you still have your job?"

"Your father is going to work for me," James said. "I've already had my architect draw up the plans for an estate on a piece of property I'm in the process of acquiring on the outskirts of Athens."

"At first, he wouldn't accept my offer to cook for him," Babá explained. "But I told him it would mean the world to me if he would allow it. So, we struck a deal, and now you're looking at the personal chef of James and Diane Morgan."

"He's going to build us a cottage on his estate," Mamá said. "I told him I don't want anything too big and fancy. But it will be our very own house. No more renting. No more apartment."

"Will I get my own room?" Nikita asked.

"Of course, you will," James said with a laugh. "I won't let our good friends live in anything less than the best."

"Nothing fancy," Mamá said again.

Gertie could tell that Mamá was as excited as Nikita to have a big house. Even though she said she didn't want anything fancy, her thoughts were of rooms as grand as the one they were standing in.

"And now, my little chickens!" Babá tickled Phoebe beneath her neck and poked Nikita in the belly. "If you will all follow me into the kitchen, I have baked the most delicious cake of my career. Come and taste for yourself!"

CHAPTER TWENTY-EIGHT

Back in Athens

The familiar honk sounded in the Morgan circular driveway. Gertie took a sip of wine from her water bottle, grabbed her backpack, kissed her mom's cheek, and headed out the door. Helios was just beginning his ascent in the early dawn on a beautiful spring day. Across the drive, the Angelis kids emerged from their house.

Although James had offered to have his driver take them to school, Hector enjoyed picking everyone up in the morning. His Mini Cooper long since destroyed in the uprising, he'd been sporting a roomier Ferrari 612 Scaglietti, so no more squeezing together in the backseat.

"Are you ready for your last day of high school?" Gertie asked Hector and Klaus as she climbed in the back with Phoebe and Nikita."

"Babá is baking you a special cake," Nikita said.

They all laughed.

"I can't wait for next year," Phoebe said. "I'll be even more popular than I am now."

"Why's that?" Hector asked from behind the wheel as he drove through the front gate.

"Because the most popular girl in school is my big sister, Gertie."

"And what am I? Chopped liver?" Nikita asked.

"No. You're the best friend of the most popular girl in school," Phoebe said.

They all laughed at Phoebe's joke. Gertie tried to imagine what it had been like during that first week in Athens, back when Phoebe didn't speak, and Gertie had no friends. Her old life was becoming harder and harder to recall. She still enjoyed her books and would never give them up, but in between series, she found herself living out her own adventures—not only as she served on the council of demigods in Athens, but also as the girlfriend of the cutest boy in town.

And at night, she left her upstairs bedroom and flew to meet Jeno at the Necromanteion, where they received their orders for the night. Usually they collected five to ten souls a night and got more than their fill of blood. In fact, Gertie felt like she was putting on a little extra weight.

Some nights she stayed home and slept in her bed, and on those evenings, she stayed up and watched television with her mom and dad. Slowly but surely, they were getting to know one another better, and getting closer, too. They planned to take a trip together over the summer, after Hector and Klaus's graduation. Her parents said that Hector could go with them.

One night, when she and Jeno had finished collecting their souls, they wandered back to the Underworld, where Jeno now lived in his own chambers lavishly decorated with the very best furnishings. The most prominent décor in Jeno's rooms consisted of clocks and timekeepers. One of these was an ancient clepsydra, similar to the one he used to have in the caves beneath the acropolis, where he and his sister Calandra had once lived. The water clock was beautiful, crafted from two bowls of pure gold trimmed with silver and decorated with copper flourishes on the base—a gift from Hephaestus. Jeno had also asked Hector to help him reproduce the paintings of his family, and Hector had done an amazing job. They hung in frames on Jeno's wall.

"I want to show you something," Jeno said.

"Okay." She followed him along the winding river of fire, past the judgment room, past Erebus and Tartarus, and all the way to the glowing Elysian Fields. Gertie had never gone this far into the Underworld, and she was amazed by the sight of all the souls frolicking in the fields of asphodel and lavender. Some read books near the Lethe streams, dangling their toes in the cool water. Others flew kites, or danced, or chased butterflies.

"They are shared illusions," Jeno told her.

"They seem happy," she said.

"Yes. And look."

She followed his finger. Sitting beneath a tree with a book in his hand was the soul of his father, Vladimir.

"He's smiling," Gertie pointed out.

"It comforts me to see him," Jeno said. "I come here every day to watch him."

"Hades allows it?"

"He hasn't interfered with anything I do."

"He must trust you. Can you talk to your father?"

"That's not allowed."

"Too bad."

"I did speak with Hades yesterday," Jeno said as they turned to go back to his rooms.

"Oh? About what?"

"I asked him how he felt about giving vampires the option of living like my father, in the fields."

Gertie's jaw dropped. "But, Jeno…"

"I'm tired. I've lived a long time."

"Jeno, please."

"I want to join my father, Gertie."

Tears pricked her eyes. "Are you serious? Are you telling me you want to *die*?"

"I want you to know I'm considering it. Hades has already given me his blessing."

Gertie put her arms around Jeno's neck and kissed his cheek. "I'm so sorry if I hurt you. I want you to know that I do love you. I love you deeply. It's just different with Hector."

"It's okay. I've already come to terms with you and Hector. I want you to be happy. That's another reason I'm considering…"

"Don't do it because of me. *Please*, Jeno! I'd rather have you alive with me than be human again."

He pushed a strand of her hair behind her ear and said, "Look over there."

She followed his finger again to see Damien chasing butterflies with Calandra beside Vladimir. More tears filled her eyes.

Although Jeno had reassured Gertie and stroked her hair and squeezed her hand, the very next day while she was sitting at Nikita's kitchen table telling her about her family's vacation plans, she felt the change.

First, Gertie froze, unable to continue speaking as the realization of what Jeno had done sunk into her head.

"What's the matter?" Nikita asked.

Tears fell from Gertie's eyes. She clutched her hands to her heart. "I think I'm going to be sick."

"What's wrong? Is it your stomach? I think there's a bug going around."

"What's the matter, Gertoula?" Mamá called from her herb garden in the next room. "Are you ill?"

"Jeno's dead," she said. "And I'm no longer a vampire."

Later that day, she convinced Hector to drive her to Parga to the Necromanteion. Nikita had pleaded to be allowed to go, too, since they would pick up Lajos in Patras first, and she didn't want to be left out. They drove to the docks in Parga, where they met Lajos and together took a boat to the temple of the dead.

On the way there, Lajos told them about populations of grizzly bears and whales that were cropping up all over the world. "Both species are being removed from the endangered list. Also, ice caps that were once melting are increasing in size again. Scientists are stumped, but global warming seems to be reversing."

Gertie took this news as a sign that Harmony had indeed been restored to Mother Earth.

Although it was not the time of year when he visited his mother, once they arrived and had entered the depts. Of the Necromanteion, Lajos called Alecto, and like last time, she first arrived in a series of blinking lights, like fireflies, before she fully appeared to them in her true form. Her snake cuddled beneath Lajos's chin as Alecto greeted her son and asked why he had come.

"I need another favor," he said.

"What is it?" she asked.

"I need to see Jeno," Gertie said. "Hector has brought his ukulele and he'll sing for the king and queen in exchange for a chance to see our friend.

"We can try," Alecto said. "Follow me."

She led them through the tunnel toward the gates where Cerberus stood guard.

"Better start singing," the Fury said.

Hector sang a song he had written after his mother had died. He felt like it now applied to Jeno, too, and to all mortal life. He called it "Time the Ender" (to hear Hector's song, go here: https://soundcloud.com/travispohler/time-the-ender):

Hold on to the time that you have left;
Time won't hold onto you.
Take what you can get from your time,
'Cause Time will take it all away from you, you...

Time, the ender.
All the time that you could have spent with her,
Taken from the hands of the sinners,

Wearing off the smiles of the grinners.

Minutes turn to hours turn to days.
How long until my whole life fades away?
Wishing for the moments that could stay,
Losing all my yesterdays.

Time, the ender.
All the time that you could have spent with her,
Taken from the hands of the sinners,
Wearing off the smiles of the grinners.

No matter how you choose to spend your time,
Wishing and regretting in your mind,
Living a life prior to your crimes,
All is ended by Time.

Hold onto the time that you have left;
Time won't hold onto you.
Take what you can get from your time,
'Cause time will take it all away from you, you...

Time, the ender.
All the time that you could have spent with her,
Taken from the hands of the sinners,
Wearing off the smiles of the grinners.

As with the last time he had sung at the gate to the Underworld, the creatures of the cave came out to listen, but Gertie could not see them as clearly with her mortal eyes. Toward the end of the song, just when Gertie feared their request would go unanswered, Hades and Persephone appeared.

Before Gertie could ask her favor, the lord of the Underworld said, "Jeno has moved on. It's time for you to do the same. Don't return, unless you intend to remain here forever."

The lord and lady vanished, Cerberus woke up, and the mortals ran for their lives.

Later that evening, at a restaurant in Patras, Gertie and Hector sat in a booth across from Nikita and Lajos with plates full of food that none of them could eat.

"It's for the best," Nikita said again. "We have to remind ourselves of that."

"I think he did it for me," Hector said to Gertie. "He told me, when we were out searching for you, that he knew how I felt about you, and he wanted us to be happy. He said he had shared thirty years with someone he truly loved, and he wanted me to have that, too."

"He did it for me," Gertie said. "He knew how I felt about you, knew that I couldn't love him the way I love you."

"Maybe he did it for himself," Lajos suggested. "Gertie, didn't you say he wanted to be with his father?"

She nodded.

"And if he *did* want the two of you to have your happily-ever-after," Nikita said, "then you better not mess it up. If he died to give you a chance at happiness, then be *happy*."

Gertie smiled first at Nikita and then at Hector. "We will. We just need time."

Hector squeezed her hand.

Later that night, Hades appeared to Gertie in a dream. "I'll let you see Jeno if you do something for me."

"Anything," Gertie said.

"I need you to return this eye to Polyphemus."

THE END

Thank you for reading my story. If you enjoyed it, please consider leaving a review. Reviews help other readers to find my books, which helps me.

Please enjoy this excerpt from the first book in my sequel series, *The Marcella II: Vampires and Gods, Book One.*

CHAPTER ONE

A Rare Find

Hestie took a deep bite of the warm September air before she dove from the deck of the *Marcella II* into the Arabian Sea. She'd swum hundreds of feet on the heels of Poros when it dawned on her that she could breathe underwater.

"I'm a goddess," she reminded herself. "I'm the goddess of languages and international relations."

And, because she could, she said those words—though they were a mouthful—in seventy-five other languages as she descended.

Poros, son of Zeus and lord of the sky, led her down—nearly ten thousand feet toward the ocean floor.

Even though it had been four weeks since she and her brother, Hermie, had become the newest gods in the pantheon, she still hadn't grown used to the liberty of not having to wear a wet suit, diving gear, or mask. The weighted belt and flippers were the only accessories she and Poros needed, besides their swimming suits and the netted crossbody bags they wore to carry their finds.

They soon reached the uneven floor and picked through sand, rocks, and seashells. Unlike the last place they'd searched a few weeks ago, this place was desolate—not a living thing in sight.

After a while, Hestie approached a boulder the size of a Volkswagen Beetle. Poros swam up behind her just as she gave it a shove, revealing the mouth of a cave.

Did you know about this? she asked him telepathically.

Poros shook his head. His hair swished in the water like the short tentacles of a yellow sea anemone. *I've never searched this spot before.*

Together they peered into the darkness. Hestie was glad for the benefit of god-sight, which enabled her to see without a dot of light.

Within a few feet of the opening, the cave veered sharply to the left. It was impossible to know where it led or what it contained without entering it.

Should we go for it? Hestie asked.

We should stay on task. Jinsoo and Captain will be here any minute and will wonder where we've gone.

She rolled her eyes. Sometimes Poros could be too much like her brother.

You stay, she said. *I'm going in.*

Her job was to look for treasure, not to explore caves, and it was unlikely that any of the treasure from the *Camille*—a ship of Prometheus's which had sunk in the Arabian Sea in the 1970's—would have made it past the giant boulder and into this small cave. Nevertheless, she swam inside to have a look around.

She wasn't surprised when Poros followed.

The opening was only a few feet in diameter. Hestie propelled herself through the tunnel by pulling on the rocky floor beneath her. This helped her to avoid scraping her back along the top of the cave as it veered right.

Bracing herself for what might be waiting just around the bend, Hestie expected to find an eel, octopus, or other sea creature hiding in the crevices of the rock, but, as she veered left and right again, she found the cave to be as desolate as the rest of the area.

It came to a dead-end in a chamber not much bigger than her bathroom on the *Marcella II*.

This would make a great hiding place, she said to Poros.

For lovers? he asked with his brows lifted.

She smirked. *For treasure.*

She swam into his arms and gave him a kiss. It wasn't easy to do underwater, but, when he cupped her cheeks and kissed her again, she tightened the embrace and enjoyed the feel of his warm body against hers.

We better go look for Jinsoo and Captain, he said.

Mood killer.

Poros laughed.

As she was about to follow him from the cave, she noticed a small wooden box—no bigger than a shoe—tucked into a crevice.

What's this? she said.

She pulled it free.

Poros returned to her side as she opened it.

She gasped, nearly choking on the sudden intake of water.

The box was filled with gold coins.

Hermie sat beside Mina on the flybridge of the *Marcella II* and grinned at the look she was giving him.

"Let's just try it," he said. "If we ruin Jinsoo's kimchi, Captain will have no choice but to take us to shore for more food. And you know what that means."

She arched a brow. "Mr. Burger?"

"Or its equivalent," he said.

"I don't know. Captain might make us starve."

"He wouldn't."

"I thought you don't need as much food, now that you a god," she said in her broken English.

Hermie sighed. "I may not need it, but a burger sure sounds good. Doesn't it? Besides, I think that kimchi is expired."

"Kimchi don't expire for a long, long time."

Hermie cocked his head to the side. "I think that's more of an ideology than a fact."

Chidori chirped, "Hilarious! Hilarious!" from where she perched on the helm.

Mina giggled, even though, being mortal, she couldn't understand the language of animals. To her, the yellow canary's sounds were nothing more than tweets.

"In orphanage, one batch of kimchi last two month," Mina said.

"You're used to it," he said. "But I'm used to hamburgers and French fries and nachos and just about anything that isn't kimchi."

Mina climbed to her feet. "Okay. Let's do it."

"Really?" Hermie hadn't thought she would agree, and, now that she had, he was having second thoughts. He didn't want to make Prometheus angry. "I don't know. Maybe it's not such a good idea."

She sank back into her chair. "No. It bad idea. Captain will be mad. He don't like waste."

"You're right," Hermie said. "How long do you think they'll be gone?"

"Two hour. Three hour." She shrugged.

"That long?"

"Why? You want to watch *Naruto*?"

"We've seen every episode."

"So?"

"Not again!" Chidori chirped.

Hermie said to Mina, "You could have gone with the others."

"I want to stay with you!"

Becoming a god hadn't changed his dislike of swimming. He'd rather avoid encounters with slimy, creepy, and sharp-toothed creatures if there were other people willing to dive in his place. He was the god of technology, after all, and he preferred to be in front of a computer screen than almost anywhere else.

He gave Mina a once-over. She looked cute in her skimpy bathing suit with her black hair tied in pigtails. She had claimed to be working on her tan, but he sensed she enjoyed showing off.

"You want to play a game?" she asked. "I can get Jinsoo's *Yu-Gi-Oh* cards. Or we could play *Urban Fighter.*"

He had a better idea but was too shy to say it.

"You want to kiss me?" she asked.

He laughed. "You read my mind. Want to sit on my lap?"

"Oooh. In Captain's chair? That funny. We make out in Captain's chair."

"Chidori, why don't you keep watch for Jinsoo and the others on the lower deck?"

"Fine," she chirped before flying away.

Hermie folded Mina onto his lap and pressed his lips to hers.

"You taste like kimchi," he said with a frown.

"Oh, stop saying kimchi and kiss me."

Unable to get past the sour taste in her mouth, he moved his lips to her neck.

"I like that," she said.

He chuckled. Every time they made out, Mina gave him a play-by-play of her feelings.

"That spot there," she said when he kissed her shoulder. "You make me crazy, Hermie!"

"But you're glad I brought you back from the dead?" he teased.

"Not again!" she said, chuckling. "How many time you want me to thank you?"

"I'm sorry. Never again."

"You said that yesterday!"

The sound of fluttering wings too large to be Chidori's made Hermie lift his head in time to see a gray owl land on the center mast.

He cleared his throat before saying, "Hello, Athena."

The owl flew from the mast to the bridge and morphed into the goddess of wisdom, her long black hair blowing away from her face as she turned her bright gray eyes on him.

"Sorry to interrupt," she said with a smile. "I have something for Poros."

She didn't look very sorry to Hermie as Mina jumped from his lap and returned to her own seat.

"He's not here," Hermie said of Athena's brother. "He's out diving."

"Is Prometheus diving, too?" Athena asked.

Hermie smiled. It wasn't the first time Athena had used her brother as an excuse to see Prometheus.

Mina nodded. "With Jinsoo. They be back in two hour or so."

"They're here! They're here!" Chidori chirped.

Just then, Prometheus emerged from the sea near the lower deck at the back of the boat, his dark curly hair and beard flattened by the water, until he shook it out like a dog, and the curls returned. Three other heads popped up with him.

Mina jumped to her feet. "They back already? That was fast!"

Athena flew to the lower deck to meet the divers. Hermie and Mina followed on foot.

"We found something!" Hestie cried as she climbed aboard.

"Oh, hi, Athena," Poros said, as he flew from the water to the lower deck.

"Hey, little brother."

Prometheus followed. "Hello, Athena. Welcome aboard."

As soon as Jinsoo climbed from the water and onto the deck, Chidori perched onto his shoulder.

Jinsoo grinned. "Hi, Chidori! Miss me?"

Chidori gave him a playful tweet.

"What did you find?" Athena asked.

Hestie took a small box from her bag and opened it.

Hermie and the others huddled close to get a view of its contents.

"Are we rich?" Mina asked.

"Those are ancient Persian darics," Athena said.

Prometheus took one from the box and turned it over in his hand. "That's exactly right. And each coin is worth over three thousand euros."

"How many coins are in there?" Jinsoo asked. "Fifty? A hundred?"

"Let's count and find out," Hestie suggested as Prometheus returned the coin to the box.

They followed Hestie up to the salon and into a u-shaped booth with windows overlooking the main deck on the bow. The teens sat around the table to help her count. Chidori remained on Jinsoo's shoulder, as usual.

While the others counted, Hermie listened to Prometheus and Athena, who were speaking together in the food prep space by the refrigerator—what to the other members of the crew was the *galley* but would always be a *kitchen* to Hermie.

"What brings you here?" Prometheus asked. "Not that you need an excuse for a visit."

"I found something else of my father's that I want Poros to have." Athena opened her palms to reveal a pair of what looked like silver cuffs. "I thought he might like these."

"Indeed." Prometheus took one of the cuffs and turned it over in his hand. "Fine white gold, is it?"

Athena shook her head. "It's adamantine. The strongest element there is—the only one that gods can't break."

"I've seen these cuffs before—on my own wrists, I believe."

"My father warded them, to prevent the wearer from conjuring weapons or from…"

"God travel. Yes, I know. Did you find his adamantine chains as well?" Prometheus asked with a frown. "The ones he used to chain me to a rock as his eagle ate my liver each day?"

"I kept those for myself, along with two other sets of cuffs just like these," she said.

"I don't think Poros will find them of any value—except sentimental, perhaps."

Athena furrowed her brows. "One never knows when one's enemies might need to be subdued."

"Your brother has no enemies."

"Don't be naïve," Athena said.

When Prometheus glanced his way, Hermie averted his eyes, back to the table and to the coin counting.

But Hermie listened as Athena added, "He's the lord of the sky and the most powerful of the Olympians. You don't think that warrants him a few enemies, especially now, while we're adjusting to the new order?"

Before Prometheus could reply, Hestie and the other teens cried out, "Sixty-seven!"

"How much is that worth, Captain?" Hestie asked.

Prometheus stepped out from behind a counter to give the coins a closer look. "I know a collector on the island of Malta who would give us a half a million euros for these coins."

"Wow!" Jinsoo cried. "That a lot, right?"

"Right," Poros said with a laugh.

"Wait a minute," Mina said. "If you are gods, why can't you *make* money? Why you dive for treasure and sell it?"

"I'm pretty sure Captain has already answered that question," Hermie said.

"Not for Mina and Jinsoo, I haven't," Prometheus said. "You see, Mina, if I create money out of nothing, the value of all money goes down."

"It's called inflation," Hermie added.

"So?" Mina said. "Who cares? More money is more money!"

"Would you rather have a hundred silver US dollars or a hundred pennies?" Hermie asked her.

"Dollars, of course!" Mina said.

"If gods make more money out of nothing, then the dollars will become pennies. They won't be worth dollars anymore. All money will go down in value."

"Oh!" she said. "I see! I see!"

"These coins will buy a lot of medical supplies and technology for communities in need," Prometheus said. "Good work, Hestie."

Hestie beamed.

"When you make me and Mina gods, Poros?" Jinsoo asked in his broken English. "It not fair, you know? My sister and I work so hard. Everything easy for you."

"Remember what I said?" Poros asked. "If you still want to become immortal on your fifteenth birthday, I'll do it then."

"That three more months," Jinsoo said.

"It's a big decision," Prometheus added.

"Are you sure that's a good idea?" Athena asked her brother. "You can't keep turning mortals into gods, Poros. There's a balance that must be maintained, and there are existing gods who will feel threatened when it's upset."

Poros's cheeks turned red. Hermie felt the blood rush to his own cheeks, too. Did Athena resent Poros for turning Hermie and Hestie into gods?

"Just these two," Poros said of Mina and Jinsoo. "No more after that. We couldn't have won against Zeus without them."

"They've got a point," Prometheus agreed.

"I suppose you can take it up with the council," Athena said. "You'll need the support of other gods to make it happen."

Poros shrugged.

"So, now what?" Athena asked. "Is the *Marcella II* heading for Malta?"

"Indeed, it is!" Prometheus smiled from ear to ear. Then he said, "Poros, pull up the anchor!"

"Yes, Captain!" Poros left for the lower deck.

"Mina and Jinsoo, prepare to hoist the mains!" Prometheus cried.

"On it, Captain!" Mina said as she followed her brother to the main deck.

"Hermie and Hestie, coil and stow the lines!"

"Yes, Captain!" Hestie said with a chuckle as she and Hermie followed the others.

As the teens prepared to sail, Prometheus and Athena flew to the flybridge.

Once they were travel-ready, Prometheus cried, "To Malta!"

CHAPTER TWO

The Best Laid Plans

H igh school was nothing compared to this," Gertie said to her best friend, Nikita, over coffee at the student center at the Athens Conservatoire.

"Tell me about it," Nikita said before taking a sip of her latte.

"At least you've had some *success*," Gertie pointed out. "Who gets cast in a musical during their first year? Nikita Angelis, ladies and gentlemen!"

"Oh, stop. It was beginner's luck. I *look* the part: dark hair, dark eyes, small, female."

"I think you just described over thirty percent of the student body."

"It's not a big part," Nikita said.

"Well, I'm flunking photography. Who flunks *photography?*" In a muttered voice she said, "Gertrude Morgan, ladies and gentlemen."

"You aren't flunking. It's only our third week. Quit being so dramatic."

"Maybe I should have auditioned for the musical," Gertie said.

They both laughed.

"Maybe not," Nikita said in between giggles.

"Seriously," Gertie said. "I don't think I can do this. I can't produce on demand. I can only do it when the muse strikes me. All these assignments and deadlines—they're ruining my mojo."

"Don't give up so soon. You just started. You'll get your groove."

Gertie took a sip of her latte. "I don't know. I was such a good student when it came to memorizing facts. Maybe I should go back to my plan of becoming a librarian."

"That wouldn't be the worst thing, since you love books."

"True. I think I would love it, actually."

Nikita's phone, which was sitting beside her cup on the table, vibrated.

"It's Lajos. Hold on." Into the phone, Nikita said, "Hey, babe!" After a beat, she frowned. "Oh, no. Okay. I'll tell her. Keep me posted, and I'll do the same."

"What's wrong?" Gertie asked.

"It's Hector. He got kicked out of the police academy and took off in his car. He wouldn't tell Klaus or Lajos where he was going. Lajos said he didn't go home."

"Oh, no." She called his number. When Hector's recorded voice played on her phone, she said, "It went straight to voice mail."

Gertie had known that Hector was struggling in the academy. They'd commiserated in the evenings together over their shortcomings in their respective fields. She'd pointed out that, as the son of Hephaestus, Hector should consider a craft. Or, since his mother was a daughter of Apollo, maybe he should go into medicine. Gertie suspected that Hector had chosen the police academy because that's what Klaus and Lajos were doing.

Maybe she had chosen the conservatoire for the same reason: to be with her friend.

She really *would* rather be a librarian. What was she doing at the Athens Conservatoire?

Gertie sent Hector a text: *Please call.*

"Do you have any idea where he might have gone?" Nikita asked her.

"Yes," Gertie said. "Let's go."

Gertie drove her new Porsche—a high school graduation gift from her parents—across town toward the acropolis. She didn't go to the acropolis proper, but along another road that led to her favorite bookstore.

"Hector's not much of a reader," Nikita said as Gertie parked the car. "Why would he come here?"

"He wouldn't." Gertie climbed from her seat. "Come on."

"Are we going to the Music Factory?"

"No. Hephaestus's Temple."

"Ah, yes. That makes sense."

The two friends hurried along the road uphill to where Hector sat on a ledge overlooking the ruins of the ancient agora—what was once the town square of Athens.

"Hey," he said as they reached him.

"Hey," the girls replied as they sat on either side of him.

"You didn't answer your phone," Gertie said.

"It died. My car charger doesn't work."

"Oh," Gertie said.

Hector glanced at Nikita. "I guess you heard."

Nikita nodded. "I'm sorry."

Gertie took his hand. "Are you okay?"

"I screwed up. I can't believe I screwed up so badly."

"What happened?" Nikita asked. "You should have been at the top of your class."

"You're right. I thought I had it in the bag. I guess I should have tried harder."

"Can't you talk to your captain?" Gertie asked.

"I did. I begged him to give me another chance."

"What did he say?" Nikita asked.

"I can try again next year."

"Oh, well, that's not so bad, then," Nikita said.

"I'd rather not waste a whole year," he said. "I've been a warrior for this city since I was twelve years old. I'm stronger and faster than any other demigod in Athens. How could I have let this happen? My mom's probably turning over in her grave."

"She's in the Elysian Fields," Gertie said.

Hector shrugged. "It's just an expression."

"It was a hard lesson," Nikita said. "But you've learned it. Now quit being a baby and move on. Where do you go from here?"

Hector shrugged again. "That's why I came up here. I was hoping for some inspiration from my father."

Gertie squeezed Hector's hand and closed her eyes to pray to any god who would listen.

They sat together in silence for many minutes as the sun prepared to set. Gertie wondered if Helios could see them sitting there, looking up at him.

Their silence was broken by a howl in the distance. On closer inspection, Gertie noticed a golden wolf bounding toward them through the ruins in the ancient agora.

Hector jumped to his feet. "Is that Apollo?"

Gertie and Nikita stood up beside Hector.

"I think so," Gertie said.

Twenty meters below them, the wolf came to a halt and transformed into a beautiful god with light brown hair—just a shade darker than Hector's and Gertie's but lighter than Nikita's—and emerald eyes that sparkled in the afternoon sunlight. He wore a quiver full of silver arrows and a bow across his back.

"I've had a vision," Apollo said. "Soon you'll be called to sea for an important cause. Be ready, Hector and Gertrude."

Then the god returned to his wolf form and barreled away.

That evening, the teens met up at Hector's house, as usual.

"Are you sure you want to do this?" Hector asked Gertie, where they sat around on couches in the living room.

Gertie held the last bottle of wine she had from Dionysus. Any wine would increase her powers, but the wine from her father gave her the special power of foresight.

"If Apollo took the trouble to tell us about his vision, it must be important," she said just before she took three gulps of the wine.

Within seconds, the room spun, and Gertie fell back against the couch cushions. Then everything around her became as black as pitch, except for one tiny spot of light across the room. She stared at the light, her entire body trembling. Her ears filled with the buzzing of bees.

As the light moved closer to her, it expanded, blocking out everything else in the room. She saw herself floating near the ceiling. Someone with long, coarse, dark curly hair was leaning over her. Gertie felt a sting at her throat before she was awash with euphoria. She watched herself across the room, floating near the ceiling, as the curly-haired person turned to look at Gertie where she lay across the couch cushions.

The curly-haired person was a girl—a vampire—with fangs dripping with Gertie's blood.

Gertie gasped.

The vision left her and was replaced by the worried faces of her friends.

"Are you okay?" Hector asked.

Gertie blinked. "Um, yeah. I think so."

"Did you see anything?" Klaus, Nikita's older brother, asked.

"Yes. I saw a vampire drinking my blood."

Gertie noticed Klaus shiver.

"I haven't seen a vampire since the uprising," Nikita said. "Aren't they serving Hades as reapers or something?"

Lajos nodded. "Most are, I think. Not all. Not all wanted that lifestyle."

"Which makes no sense," Klaus said. "They're guaranteed blood from a fresh corpse just before they deliver the soul to Charon. What vampire wouldn't want that? It's better than living in caves and tricking unsuspecting mortals, like in the old days."

"Or preying on mortals who become addicted to their powers," Nikita added.

Gertie felt the blood leave her face. That had been her just over a year ago. She'd loved the feeling that the vampire virus gave her during the six hours it was in her system after being bitten. She'd been addicted to the powers of flight, invisibility, strength, and mind control. Specifically, she'd been addicted to Jeno, though, at the time, she thought it was love.

She still wondered if it might have been both.

"We all agreed that forced servitude would be wrong," Hector reminded them. "So, naturally, a few outliers will go their own way. There's still at least a dozen vampires who hang out in the streets of downtown Athens at night and sleep in caves beneath the acropolis during the day."

Gertie shivered at memories of Jeno and his sister, Calandra.

Nikita leaned closer to Gertie. "Do you think your vision is related to Apollo's?"

"I don't know," she said.

"You saw nothing related to the sea?" Klaus asked.

Gertie shook her head.

Nikita turned to Lajos. "Hey, babe. Do you think your mom might know anything?"

"I suppose it's possible," Lajos said. "I'm supposed to visit her next month, but I could go sooner."

"That would be great," Nikita said. "Can we all go? All five of us?"

A few days later, on Saturday afternoon, Gertie drove her friends from Athens to Parga. Along the way, she told them bits and pieces she had learned about Alecto since the last time she had seen her.

"According to Hesiod," Gertie said to her friends from behind the wheel, "Alecto is a fan of snakes. So, I thought she might enjoy this pair of earrings I found at a boutique near the acropolis."

"Cool!" Nikita said.

"That was nice of you," Lajos said. "But I can tell you what you want to know about my mother. You don't have to conduct research."

"Do you know me at all?" Gertie said with a laugh.

"Obviously not," Hector said from the passenger's seat. "Let her do her research. She gets irritable if she can't be the expert in all things."

Gertie punched Hector playfully on the shoulder. "Not true."

"Yeah, right," Nikita said laughing.

"Are you guys saying I'm a know-it-all?" Gertie asked.

"Your words, not mine," Hector said before he kissed her cheek.

They stopped for dinner around five o'clock in Agrinio and arrived at dusk at the marina, where they rented a boat.

This was the first time Gertie had returned since her friend Jeno had died. As they reached the end of the dock, where their rental was waiting, she wiped a tear from her cheek.

"You okay?" Hector asked as he helped her onto the boat.

She nodded and sat on the bench behind the captain's chair. Nikita sat between her and Lajos. Klaus took the swivel seat at the front of the boat, and Hector, who had the most experience operating boats, took the captain's chair, where he brought the engine to life.

"This is supposed to be a fun adventure," Nikita said beside her. "Lighten up."

Gertie shrugged. "I don't have a good feeling about this."

It took them half an hour to reach the place where the Acheron met the Cocytus River near the ruins of the Necromanteion—an ancient temple devoted to Hades and Persephone. Darkness had fallen, along with a chill that made Gertie shiver as they docked the boat and climbed ashore. Using the flashlight app on their phones to guide them, the five teens followed the lonely path to the ruins.

Lajos, whose vibrant red hair seemed brighter in the moonlight, led them to an underground tunnel. Below them was an uneven path, but above them were beautiful stone arches evenly spaced like something one would find in an ancient castle. They followed the tunnel until it came to a cave glistening with moonlight that shone through cracks above them onto a pool of water at their feet.

They stopped at the edge of the pool.

"I'll call my mom," Lajos said as he closed his eyes and lifted his palms.

Gertie and Nikita exchanged glances. Gertie knew Nikita was nervous, as she should be. Alecto the Unceasing was a terrifying Fury who punished the souls of evildoers in Tartarus. They'd met Lajos's mother a year ago during the vampire uprising. The meeting hadn't been long, but it had been long enough. Gertie wondered if Lajos planned to introduce Nikita as his girlfriend.

"Here," Gertie said as she handed the earrings to Nikita. "You should give them to her."

"Thanks." Nikita forced a smile, though she was clearly scared to death.

From across the pool, a set of twinkling lights, like fireflies, appeared and floated toward them. Once they were less than twenty feet away, the goddess appeared. Her golden eyes were fierce, and her red hair was spiked. Her face was pale and beautiful, like an artfully chiseled statue. A thick snake curled around her neck, poised to strike.

Gertie wondered where her wings were. The last time Alecto had appeared to them, she'd worn pale green wings, shaped like the wings of a bat.

"Mother," Lajos said. "Thank you for coming."

"I'm glad to see you, Lajos," the Fury said. "But I'm alarmed. You're early. Is something wrong?"

"Apollo appeared to Gertie, Hector, and Nikita," Lajos said. "You met them last year, remember?"

"Indeed," the goddess said.

Gertie wasn't sure if she should say hello or keep quiet, so she gave the goddess a nod as Lajos continued.

"Apollo said that he'd had a vision in which Hector and Gertie were called to sea for an important mission. Do you know anything about this?"

"No, I'm afraid not. I can ask around. Hecate might know. She has visions, too."

Gertie sighed, hiding her disappointment.

"Thank you," Lajos said.

The Fury moved closer and put a hand on her son's shoulder. "It's so good to see you. I worry about you, with your father gone. Would you be terribly frightened if I came to visit you now and then?"

"Frightened? I'd be happy, Mother. I'm always happy to see you." Lajos kissed her cheek.

The goddess smiled at Lajos and then turned to Hector. "Thank you for being a friend and for inviting him to share your home."

Hector bowed as he said, "It's my pleasure, goddess."

Then she turned to Nikita. "And you, my dear."

Nikita gave the Fury a hopeful smile.

"If you break my son's heart, I'll break your neck."

Nikita's mouth and eyes became wide.

Then Alecto laughed. It sounded like a cackle. "I'm only joking."

Gertie chuckled but Nikita's face remained pale.

"For you, goddess," Nikita said as she held out the earrings.

"How beautiful. Thank you." Alecto took the gift and turned to his son. "Are you still enjoying the police academy?"

"I love it. It feels like it's what I was meant to do."

Gertie wanted to give Hector's hand a reassuring squeeze but thought her pity would make him feel worse, so she didn't.

"I'm glad to hear that," Alecto said. "You'll make a fine officer."

"How are things in Tartarus?" Lajos asked.

"Busy." Alecto laughed.

Gertie and her friends laughed, too.

"Do more people end up there than in the Elysian Fields?" Nikita asked.

"No, but many people start there," Alecto said. "Before they move on to the fields, they need to be purged of their guilt and regret."

"Does that take a long time?" Klaus asked.

"More for some than others," Alecto said with a grin.

Then Klaus said, "Would it be possible for us to see the form you take in Tartarus?"

"Be careful what you ask for," Alecto said.

"Please?" Gertie asked.

Alecto combed her fingers through her spiky, red hair. "I'd hate to make my son afraid of me."

"That would never happen," Lajos said.

"Okay, then," Alecto said. "You asked for it."

Her spiky hair transformed into dozens of red snakes, with red eyes, fangs, and slithering tongues. Alecto's eyes were equally red, with blood dripping from them. Green wings, as thin as paper, emerged from her back. Each wing had a green claw on its tip. Her hands also became claws, and when she opened her mouth, it was filled with sharp teeth.

Gertie and her friends took several steps back from the horrifying sight. It was only a few seconds before Alecto returned to her beautiful form, but it had been long enough to leave a lasting feeling of terror in Gertie's chest. From the expressions on her friends' faces, she suspected they felt the same.

Even Lajos was no longer smiling.

"I warned you," Alecto said. "But don't forget how important my work is. People who do bad things would never find peace if it weren't for me and my sisters."

"I know that, Mom," Lajos said. "It was just a shock, that's all."

"I thought you looked sexy as hell," Klaus said with a smile.

"Klaus!" Nikita punched her brother's shoulder.

Alecto laughed. "I need to get back to work."

"Thanks for meeting me." Lajos took Nikita's hand as his mother turned to go.

"I'll come to you if I learn anything about Apollo's prophecy," the Fury said before she vanished into a collection of sparkling lights.

"Sorry, guys," Lajos said, once they were alone in the quiet cave. "I guess this was a waste of time for you."

"Are you kidding?" Klaus said. "It's never a waste of time to see a goddess, especially one as badass as your mother."

"It wasn't a waste," Hector agreed as they followed the tunnel in the direction from which they had come. "Your mom will ask around for us, and maybe she'll learn something."

EVA POHLER

Eva Pohler is a *USA Today* bestselling author of over thirty novels in multiple genres, including mysteries, thrillers, and young adult paranormal romance based on Greek mythology. Her books have been described as "addictive" and "sure to thrill"—*Kirkus Reviews*.

To learn more about Eva and her books, and to sign up to hear about new releases, and sales, please visit her website at www.evapohler.com.

Made in the USA
Middletown, DE
31 December 2021

57144236R00142